with no days, the exquisite *A Sunday in Ville-d'Avray*
captures the haunted feeling of a bygone Sunday, the
already too late, and the bittersweet homesickness of
end. This wistful novel, a sunbeam illuminating the
moments of someone else's ordinary tragedy, will
ou for weeks."

—Barbara Bourland, author of *Fake Like Me*
and *I'll Eat When I'm Dead*

Dominique Barbéris's novel conjures the smell of grass
f dead leaves burning in a backyard, the mild, melan-
s of the Parc de Saint-Cloud at the start of autumn."
—*Sud Ouest*

ling text on memory and the marks of regret…a
a singular evocative power."
—*Le Monde des livres*

pheric novel plunges us into the folds of our own emo-
s to a richly evocative style…It has the troubling mel-
Modiano's novels and the charm of Rohmer's films."
—*Gael*

PRA

A Sunday i

"An exquisite inquiry into t
eloquent, and tinged with d
Sunday. Simply, I loved this
—Erika Sw

"Quiet but suspenseful, A S
of two sisters. As one sist
years before, the other's p
atmospheric and brooding
regrets, images of Paris a
evoking the psychological
Brookner. Perfect for fans

"The experience of A Sur
a novel and more like fa
a life both familiar and d
immersive. If you are a F
if you live in the suburbs
this book is for you."
—Eliza

"In a
pred
afte
a me
rain
stay

"Supe
after
choly

"An u
novel

"This a
tions t
anchol

A Sunday in Ville-d'Avray

A Sunday
in Ville-d'Avray

DOMINIQUE BARBÉRIS

Translated from the French by John Cullen

OTHER PRESS
New York

Copyright © Arléa, 2019
English translation copyright © Other Press, 2021
Originally published in 2019 as *Un dimanche à Ville-d'Avray* by Arléa, Paris

Production editor: Yvonne E. Cárdenas
Text designer: Jennifer Daddio Bookmark Design & Media Inc.
This book was set in Goudy Old Style and Carlton by
Alpha Design & Composition of Pittsfield, NH.

1 3 5 7 9 10 8 6 4 2

Library of Congress Cataloging-in-Publication Data
Names: Barbéris, Dominique, author. | Cullen, John, 1942- translator.
Title: A Sunday in Ville-d'Avray : a novel / Dominique Barbéris ;
translated from the French by John Cullen.
Other titles: Dimanche à Ville-d'Avray. English
Description: New York : Other Press, [2021] | Originally published in 2019 as
Un dimanche à Ville-d'Avray by Arléa, Paris.
Identifiers: LCCN 2020038362 (print) | LCCN 2020038363 (ebook) |
ISBN 9781635420456 (hardcover) | ISBN 9781635420463 (ebook)
Classification: LCC PQ2662.A6518 D5613 2021 (print) | LCC PQ2662.A6518 (ebook) |
DDC 843/.914—dc23
LC record available at https://lccn.loc.gov/2020038362
LC ebook record available at https://lccn.loc.gov/2020038363

For

Anne Bourguignon

The other Sunday, I went to see my sister.

My *sister lives in Ville-d'Avray*, in the western suburbs of Paris. She shares a comfortable house with Christian, her husband, and their daughter: big garden, with lawns and flower beds, in a residential neighborhood. One of those streets that climb the hills near the Parc de Saint-Cloud. As I live in the center of Paris, we seldom see each other and I rarely visit her. Luc says, "Going to see your sister is an expedition."

But that's not true, the distance isn't the only issue. I know very well that there's regular train service to Ville-d'Avray. The truth is that Luc doesn't like Ville-d'Avray, and that he finds my sister "boring"; it would

1

be more accurate to say that he's suspicious of her. Her husband Christian's a physician in a group practice. For a brief time she was a high school teacher, like me, but she doesn't work anymore. She helps Christian in his practice, in a vague sort of way. Sometimes, when he needs her, she fills in at the reception desk, treats people with ordinary symptoms over the phone, or directs anxious patients to the hospital, but that's not what you'd call work. "And between us," says Luc, "I don't trust your sister's ability to diagnose patients; she always seems to be 'elsewhere.' Your sister," says Luc, "has never had her feet on the ground. It's a family trait."

At that point Luc and I usually have an argument. We have an argument every time we talk about our respective families.

As I was leaving Paris that Sunday, I calculated how many months it had been since we'd last spoken to each other, my sister and I. Luc was attending a seminar, or claimed to be attending a seminar. I had my doubts on the subject. To be more precise, for some time I'd been suspicious of his relationship with a woman from our circle of friends, Fabienne, an academic. In any case, I'd had enough of Paris; the city was hot and polluted.

The season was moving on. It was, I remember, a Sunday in the beginning of September, one of those days that cross the border between summer and fall.

Some of the houses in the neighborhoods I passed through were still closed up—proof that their owners hadn't yet returned from summer vacation—but there were flowers in the gardens. Flowers blooming in untended gardens, all by themselves. You could sense everywhere, much more than in Paris, the sort of languid stretching and immobility characteristic of plants in the fall. There were fewer red roses than pale-pink ones—red roses, despite their more pronounced color and their stronger scent, don't last as long. They seem to wear themselves out.

Maybe it's the color that wears out the roses.

I passed a station, I don't remember which one, where the people getting off a train from Paris stood out behind the railing that separated the platform from the street like figures silhouetted against a background of sky. You got the impression that they were hesitating, they didn't know where to go. The train left again; it was typical of Sunday, all that, the degree of blankness, of slight uncertainty, of vague apprehension (connected

3

to uncertainty) that characterizes a Sunday; I put on my sunglasses and told myself that despite the fine weather, despite what was left of summer, you could always recognize a Sunday afternoon.

On Sunday evenings when my sister and I were children and our family lived in Brussels, Mama was often nervous. Night fell faster than it did on the other days of the week, especially in winter, and it was preceded by a damp fog. We'd be brought to the park; we'd be required to walk around the lake, to "get some fresh air." "Walk fast and breathe through your noses—if you don't, you'll inhale the dampness, you'll get sore throats, and I have no intention of taking care of you." We'd go up on the Japanese bridge and throw bread to the swans. Mama would watch us from a distance, clutching her fur collar tight with both gloved hands. On the avenue that bordered the park, the streetlamps would come on one by one; we liked the way those lights, magnified by the foggy mist, shone in the night; we could feel their chilly poetry, but on the way back we'd walk "as though we were walking on eggshells," with a strange pang in our hearts. We knew what the rest of the evening would be like. It was the same every

4

Sunday: when we got back home, Mama would re-proach Papa, who'd stayed home to read the newspaper, for the boredom and the household chores with which marriage had filled her life. Those reproaches were ex-acerbated by our life in Belgium; our life in Belgium greatly exacerbated the Sunday evening anxiety in our home. For example, the neighbors in the apartment above ours, a Belgian couple (the Kacenelenbogens), were content with café au lait and *tartines de cassonade*, slices of bread spread with butter and brown sugar, for Sunday dinner. From this practice Mama would draw an argument: if we could only have been Belgians, real Belgians, free from French complications in matters regarding *la cuisine*, we would have eaten *tartines de cassonade* like the Kacenelenbogens, and she wouldn't have had to tire herself out. She'd slam the kitchen door; she'd say that Sundays were unbearable, and that her life was a failure.

As for the neighbors below us (the Van Huysts), they had made some comments on the noise coming from the floor above their heads. We were required to wear slippers with felt soles inside the apartment. Sometimes we'd pretend to skate on the floor in the hall, as if on a Dutch canal. We'd go over our poems. Monday was recitation day, so we always went over our poems the night before. I haven't forgotten the ones we learned; they seemed fitting for Sunday, for the gray, cloudy weather. There was the one that started, "Here's the wind, the wild November wind," and also one by Théophile Gautier called "Autumn Song":

Rain bubbles on the garden pond.
The swallows gathered on the roof
Confabulate and correspond.

Reciting the poems gave me a delicate pleasure, delicate and a little sad.

Our apartment was very silent. The silence would weigh on us, and we'd ask permission to turn on the television set and watch Thierry la Fronde, Terry the Sling. In those days, like all the girls of our generation, we were in love with Thierry la Fronde; I'm tempted to say like all the *normal* girls of our generation, but sometimes I wonder if our childhood, my sister's and mine, was normal.

No one's childhood is really normal, I suppose.

———

Speaking of Thierry la Fronde, a good many years ago I saw the actor Jean-Claude Drouot onstage, in a performance of Chekhov's play *Uncle Vanya.* Drouot played the title role, but it was hard to believe him. He wore the rumpled white linen suit that in the imagination of French directors represents the way Russian landowners dressed in summer on their birch-wooded estates. He had aged, which shocked me; even so, he didn't look at all like a Russian landowner. He looked as though he was still roaming, with his jerkin, his sling, and his companions, through the forests of French public television (ORTF, as it was in our day). It was a weird feeling that lasted, in my case, for the whole performance, as if Chekhov's melancholy had suddenly replaced the memory of our Sunday afternoons in front of the television.

I was sitting in the third row of the orchestra, and while the play was going on, I spoke to the actor in my mind. I said to him, *You just can't fool us.*

(Or was it *You just can't make us forget?*)

We had tender hearts and lots of imagination.

Two or three years later, Jane Eyre's alarming "master," the formidable and gloomy Mr. Rochester, succeeded

Terry the Sling. Rochester too appeared to us on the small screen one afternoon, in an old Hollywood adaptation of the novel. He made such an impression that I can still see him arriving, a horseman riding on the fog, his burly silhouette, his cape like a Gothic king's, his curly black hair, which he pushes off his pale forehead as he asks, "*Jane, do you find me handsome?*"

The answer floored us: "*No*," Jane boldly says.

That was surely on a Sunday (Sunday was television day). The living room was filled with late afternoon darkness. Crows were circling the chimneys of Thornfield; sounds of rattling chains echoed in the corridors. Our knees were weak, our eyes bulging, our mouths slightly open, when Mama opened the door: "Close your mouths, don't slump on the sofa. Have you learned your recitations? I want to hear you recite in ten minutes."

We were going to recite "The Wild November Wind" and "Rain bubbles on the garden pond." But it was too late; the damage had been done; it would last. Thierry la Fronde, newly perceived as dull and scrawny, got tossed into the dustbin of childhood. Now we dreamed of being afraid; we dreamed of a gloomy man our father's age, with wide nostrils, Orson Welles's head (Welles played Rochester), and the look of a half-caste king.

There was one scene we were especially fond of: Jane's spoiled wedding. It would suggest to my sister the scenario of a game that I describe here to give an idea of what our childhood was like (and which, naturally, I keep secret from Luc): it consisted in wrapping ourselves up in one of the transparent curtains that decorated the window in our room. This window, situated just above the radiator, overlooked the courtyard of our apartment building, a courtyard where there was absolutely nothing to see: some garages and the roofs of other buildings, bristling with TV antennas. Nobody could guess what we were doing. Or—to be fair—people outside could naturally suppose we were misbehaving. They could figure we were sunk in the glum and guilty boredom of children, the boredom of Sunday evenings.

Nothing was further from the truth: our hearts were pounding because we'd just put on our "wedding veils." Unmoving and veiled, our noses in the sheer curtains, which smelled (I remember) like dust and new fabric, our knees hot from the radiator, singing softly (a diversionary tactic), we'd stand in spirit "before the altar," *betrothed*, hand in hand with a gloomy, "olive-skinned," no-longer-young man.

"Does anyone know of an impediment to this marriage?" the priest would ask.

A voice would cry out from the back of the church: "Stop! The marriage cannot take place. Mr. Rochester has a living wife."

"Proceed," Rochester would say to the clergyman.

He'd bring us back to the manor house, squeezing our hands in his "grasp of iron." He'd open the door to the hidden room, guarded by a certain Grace Poole, and reveal to us his secret: a woman kept under lock and key, a disgusting red-faced gorgon with unkempt hair, neighing like a beast, our rival.

"That is my wife," he'd say; "Such is the sole conjugal embrace I am ever to know . . . And this is what I wished to have," turning toward us, "this young girl, who stands so grave and quiet at the mouth of hell."

That's what we were doing, my sister and I, under the curtains on Sunday evenings. We were standing, grave and quiet, at the mouth of hell.

"Why is it so dark in here? What on earth are you two doing, always tangled up in those curtains? These

children are nervous wrecks," Mama cried when she opened the door. "When are you going to start your homework? If you don't study, you'll end up cashiers. Discount store cashiers. So you know what's waiting for you."

Those were the days when my sister developed a taste for spending long periods of time at the window, doing nothing. This soon turned into a habit.

She had such a capacity for silence that it sometimes upset Mama: "What's Claire Marie doing? I can't hear her. Go see what she's up to. She's not going to look out the window all day long."

I knew very well what Claire Marie was up to when she had her nose pressed against the glass: she was wandering the moors, pouring buckets of water on Rochester's burning bed, strolling with him in the orchard at twilight (*"Jane, do you hear that nightingale?"*), or she was in one of the rooms in Thornfield Hall in the dead of night, sponging blood off a stranger—an operation that fascinated us, by the way. When we were asked to clean the table (which we had to do after supper every night, taking turns), we'd watch the sponge swell up with water; we had a vague notion of what it might be like to "sponge away blood." A stranger's blood.

I'd ask the question for appearances' sake, in my capacity as interpreter of the Higher Powers: "What are you doing?" I'd say to my sister.

"Nothing," my sister would reply.

"Nothing," I'd go back and tell the said Powers.

"She doesn't have homework to do? She doesn't have any math exercises? How does she expect to make any progress? That child's going to wind up being a cashier! She won't be able to say no one warned her!"

I remember a phase when we were totally somnambulant, when we were conducting a nonstop amorous discourse. We'd walk, sleep, comb our dolls' hair, and talk to Rochester all the while. We thought we could hear him calling in the night.

"Is that you? Where are you, Master?"

We had begged for the book, we were reading it, at night, in bed with the lights out, embroidering the plot, inventing scenes that thrilled us and frightened us.

("Those children are going to wind up with myopia, both of them!")

—————

I believe my sister stayed under the spell of that literary love affair for a long time, while I, younger but clearly more practical-minded, developed a crush on my first-year Latin teacher, Monsieur Jumeau (Bernard Jumeau). My grades climbed up to the heights. I knew my declensions by heart. I worked hard to dazzle him. Things went so far that predictions for my future employment shifted from cashier to Latinist or archivist-paleographer—which had been Monsieur Jumeau's first vocation and fondest dream; he told us about it in the course of a gathering in the faculty room. Blushing and modest, I stood between my parents the whole time. I was twelve. He suggested the same future for me, a suggestion I took as a declaration of reciprocal love and a discreet way of making our engagement official.

"*Very nice, your Latin teacher,*" Mama said when we got home from the party. "And a pretty good-looking man."

—————

IN THE END, I didn't study archival paleography.

On the road to Ville-d'Avray that day many years later, in the immobility of that fall Sunday, I nevertheless gave some brief thought—and why? Was it an intuition? Was it because I was moving closer to my sister?—to Monsieur Jumeau (Bernard Jumeau). He had dark hair; he looked (at least in my personal mythology) like the statue of Julius Caesar *Imperator* reproduced in our Latin textbook. He'd been my first incursion into the domain of real feelings and actual life. It was obvious that Thierry la Fronde or Rochester couldn't be considered in the same way. Then I said to myself, *Have no regrets! If you'd pursued your studies in archival paleography, you'd surely be myopic by now. Archivist-paleographers have to spend hours and hours in the library.*

As for Claire Marie, she made a late exit from her Rochester period and plunged straight into her rock music period. A taste for acrobatic rock'n'roll replaced a taste for daydreaming. Or, more precisely, her musical enthusiasms alternated for a good while with her other phases, which tended to be more fanciful. Young, long-haired rock'n'rollers, energetic fellows whose handshakes were vigorous and upbeat, just the way Papa

14

loathed them, succeeded one another in her heart. Periodically, when Mama returned from one of her evenings out, she'd go back to predicting a future as a cashier for Claire Marie and, because she wouldn't be able to keep a steady job, the general failure of her life.

AND SO I WAS FULL OF MEMORIES, I was in the melancholy state of mind that often comes over me when I go to see my sister, and I think I started by getting a little lost in Ville-d'Avray, by driving through the provincial, peaceful streets of my sister's neighborhood, past private homes with their gleaming bay windows, their porches, their phony airs (Art Deco villa, Norman country house), their gardens planted with rosebushes and cedars.

I had the good luck to find a parking spot on her street. The doorbell at the gate emitted two or three rising notes. Nobody came; but an upstairs window was open.

After five minutes or so, my sister stuck her nose out the front door, cried out in surprise, and crossed the garden to the gate. Her bare feet were in flip-flops, she wore no makeup, her hair was disheveled; she seemed a bit distracted; she pushed a thick lock of hair off her forehead, and I thought I heard Mama (or Grandma) say, "Comb your hair for a change, Claire Marie!"

I asked her, "Are you by yourself? Am I disturbing you?"

"Not at all," my sister said. "I was reading, and I must have dozed off. You're not disturbing me at all. I don't see you that often, you know. It's a surprise. Especially on a Sunday!" She gave a slight laugh. "You and Luc didn't go out for a walk? Everybody takes a walk on Sunday. Especially since the fine weather won't last. The house isn't very tidy at the moment. Don't look at my cellar. It's a shambles!"

Music was coming from one of the rooms.

"Mélanie's playing the piano, rehearsing for her audition. And Christian's at the office, he's on duty today, it's his turn. I think he'll be home late. We'll sit in the garden."

She showed me the dry soil under her rosebushes. "I shouldn't have fallen asleep, I should have watered the roses. You see, we just came back from vacation, the garden needs a lot of attention. This Sunday's half over, and I still haven't got anything done. It's terrible. Soon it'll be time to deal with the leaves. It's been very dry, so they've already started falling, and when they fall, they pile up. Stay there, I'm going to get us something to drink and tell Mélanie you're here."

She walked toward the house, making a broad gesture that meant, *Things are piling up. Leaves are piling up.* As if she were helpless in the face of those enormous piles.

I could hear my niece's piano through the window. Her room was on the upper floor; I'd seen her open window; it looked out on a cedar that hid the house across the street. From time to time, my niece stopped playing. There was a passage that kept tripping her up, but when that happened, she'd dutifully start the whole piece over. Through her open window, she must have been breathing the still air, full of the peace proper to the beginning of autumn, full of its damp tranquillity. Her neighbor was mowing his lawn; the loud drone of his motor competed with the piano; I imagined my niece turning toward the window in irritation from time to time as she played. She surely dreamed of being an elegant, refined pianist whom men would admire. And she was, perhaps, in love with her piano teacher. Classic.

Unfortunately, the piano teacher would say, "That's not very good, not very good at all."

Life's like that: you make a valiant effort to carry your dreams, yours or those of others.

As I WAITED IN THE GARDEN, I also had a familiar but indefinable feeling, slightly heavy, like a mild illness. Ville-d'Avray is just a few minutes from Paris, but you'd think you were hundreds of kilometers away. That, no doubt, explains how a man like Luc can be incapable of comprehending the universe my sister lives in. Luc's the very model of a busy, active Parisian. He's stuffed full of theories about all sorts of things; he's adaptable, practical, rational, often ironic. He has reasoned opinions on every subject. I've often tried to explain to him that this is not the case with Claire Marie. Not that she isn't intelligent. She's read a lot, but she hasn't drawn any theories from all that reading. She's remained muddleheaded, dreamy, passive. I'm sure that Ville-d'Avray, with its peaceful, secluded streets, its houses set back in their gardens, given over to the passage of the seasons as if defenseless against time, has further increased the gap between her and reality. She has all sorts of outdated habits: every time I invite her to my house, she "dresses up": I'm sure she tries on several of the dresses in her closet, I'm sure she hesitates, like Mama, and asks Christian, who's waiting for her and hurrying her along, asks him the way Mama would ask Papa, "Are you sure this looks all right on me? Wouldn't the little blue dress be prettier?" Whereupon she takes out "the little blue dress" and says, "I'll just slip it on, won't take a second, and you'll tell me what you think." And then she changes her mind and tries on something else and complains, "I don't have anything to wear, I can't, I won't be good enough"; she's afraid of not being "good enough," but one might well wonder why; her indecisiveness is obsessive. Result: she always arrives late and her hair's a mess, but she's decorated "like a flowerpot" (one of Luc's expressions for her). Most of our friends, Parisian academics, come to our parties wearing jeans, a manifestation of their critical spirit, of their free outlook on life; a sign that they've liberated themselves from the tiresome, bourgeois ceremonial of appearances. It would be more accurate to say that the ceremonial takes subtler forms in their case, hidden in certain nearly invisible details of their clothes, which are simple, well-tailored, usually black, responsive to selective codes, born in the center of Paris, fluctuating like fashion, and which my sister does not own *because* she lives in Ville-d'Avray.

"What did you think about Claire Marie's dress?" Luc asks me when the party's over and we're back in our bedroom. He sounds critical. "Where does she buy her clothes?"

When she's at our house, she seems about as comfortable as an owl that's left the woods; she makes the rounds from group to group, courteously holds out her hand to our friends, shows nothing, rarely takes part in the conversation; I think what's being said leaves her indifferent.

It sometimes happens that one of our guests notices her and later asks me a question: "Who was the tall, thin woman in red at your place the other day?"

"My sister," I say. "My older sister."

"One doesn't see much of her."

Then I say, "She lives in Ville-d'Avray." Which isn't an explanation.

"She's got something, not that I know what it is," our friend Adrien pointed out one day, he who prides himself on his psychological insights and his amorous successes. "She looks like Faye Dunaway. The tall dark-haired guy's her husband?"

"An old actress who must be well past it at this point." That was Luc's comment when I told him about the conversation. "But you know Adrien, he's a smooth talker."

To be honest, I think I can assert that the vague discomfort I felt that day as I waited in the garden was the same as the malaise I often experience when we're invited to Ville-d'Avray for lunch on a spring Sunday. In those cases, Claire Marie calls me up and says, "Come and enjoy the garden, we'll eat outdoors. We'll do a barbecue."

She imagines that we, like all Parisians, suffer from lack of fresh air and greenery. But that's a mistake: Luc loves the atmosphere of the boulevards, he loves the cafés in the Latin Quarter, they cause him no suffering at all.

Those days at my sister's start off well but end with the same uneasy, slightly odd feeling. All the same, lunch is pleasant. The weather's lovely. The table's set with paper napkins. I go inside to join Claire Marie in the kitchen and help her with the aperitifs while Luc and

Christian (we say "the men") stay in the garden, in the shade of the big cedar. They're relaxing, we tell each other, my sister and I, they're calm, they're "among themselves." We pretend to believe they're discussing some topic or other, but the truth is, they don't do discussions. Luc gets bored. Afterward, he says that Ville-d'Avray depresses him. Christian cooks slices of beef on the barbecue. The barbecue's in the back of the garden, and we watch him standing in the greasy smoke, sticking his big fork into the meat and turning it over on the grill. From across the yard, he asks us, "Medium or well done?"

Little by little, as the afternoon progresses, we're seized by an anxiety that has no apparent cause. Pollen settles on our coffee cups. Wind blows the paper napkins onto the grass. Luc kicks me, more than once, under the table so that I'll give the departure signal. Driving home, he keeps his eyes straight ahead, says nothing, and looks gloomy—which is not a good sign. At last he blurts it out: "Frankly, if I had to live all year round in Ville-d'Avray, I'd kill myself!"

I don't reply. I think I know what he means to say, or rather what he's escaping from at such high speed:

those neatly aligned gardens, each with its number; those numbered lives that go on, once the house is in place, in the contemplative silence of the garden, until the little hitch—which is, after all, inevitable—occurs: the day when the doctor comes in with the "bad results," when the doctor says further tests will have to be performed; when time, which has been slowly flowing along—punctuated by the flowering of the lilacs (my sister has one in her garden), the rather dreary neglect of the summer days when everyone's on vacation, the collecting of the fallen leaves, the filling of the boiler, the maintenance of the English lawn, closely mown and sponge-soft—when all that suddenly seems to tip over into the void yawning just behind it.

Very often, during such afternoons, I observe my sister on the sly, wondering if she feels what we're feeling. She doesn't look unhappy. But with her you never can tell. As we're leaving, I always say, "It was delightful! How pleasant your garden is! How lucky you two are!" But something shows me she's not fooled. Every time she leaves a gathering at my house, she declares, "You have such nice friends!" Yet it's quite clear to me that she doesn't think so at all.

I even remember a conversation we had years ago. Claire Marie abruptly turned to me and asked, in her direct, slightly ingenuous way, "Are there ever times when you dream of something else?"

"What do you mean, something else?"

"I don't know, I . . . ," my sister sighed. "Does your life satisfy you?"

I said, "Yes, why? Everything's fine."

I have to be honest: that wasn't true. I'd felt it the moment I said it; my relationship with my sister, I must admit, is much more ambiguous than it appears to be. Her question had stirred up something buried in a secret corner of my mind (or my heart), the old, vague, passionate dream, the never-forgotten images of an overblown, schmaltzy romanticism: the pasteboard reproduction of the manor house, the flames of the fire, the drama, the banks of artificial fog, and looming up from them, "Orson Welles," the dashing cavalier, the ideal man, the tormented "master"!

It was a remnant of childhood, I knew it. Our life with Rochester—my sister's and mine—isn't acceptable to anyone; our childhood isn't acceptable to anyone. It weighs on us. But we can't manage to get rid of it. It makes us exiles. I've tried to conceal it, I try to bluff. I try to appear liberated and modern (not an easy goal to accomplish, you have to admit, given the heavy burden of our upbringing on my sister and me). I've tried with all my strength to adjust.

That was why I resented my sister. That's what's so irritating about her. She rattles you. Our conversation upset me so much that I brought it up that very evening: "You know what Claire Marie asked me?" I said to Luc, quite casually. "She wanted to know if I didn't dream of something else, if my life 'satisfies me.'"

I was ensconced on the bed, painting my toenails. Luc was in the bathroom; I couldn't see his reaction. He didn't answer me, and so, sitting there on the bed with my toes spread apart, contemplating the ten little red rectangles while waiting for the nail polish—Rouge Passion, carefully chosen at the Champs-Élysées Sephora— to dry, I wondered whether he'd heard me. Or maybe he was brushing his teeth. The water was running in the sink. I don't like to hear water running. I get the feeling that time is passing, that the globe's resources are being used up. I get the feeling I'm losing something.

———

I called out, "Can't you turn off the faucet? Do you hear me?" And then, "What do you think about what I just told you?"

I hardly dare reveal the answer I was waiting for. I'm ashamed of it. I was waiting for the wind-buffeted moor to replace the bathroom corridor. I was waiting for a dashing cavalier to emerge from it and take me in his arms and press me against him *"like a frightened little bird."* I was waiting for him to say to me, *"Jane, sometimes I feel as if I had a string somewhere under my left ribs, tightly knotted to a similar string somewhere in your chest. And if that cord of communion should snap, Jane, I have a nervous notion I would take to bleeding inwardly."*

"What do you expect?" Luc said, coming out into the corridor in his pajamas and standing under the hall light with his toothbrush in his hand. "You know very well how your sister is. That's just pure Ville-d'Avray."

So that's what I was thinking about that day as I lounged on my sister's chaise longue. I was facing her house, and I wondered for a brief moment when she would turn on the outside light and if little mosquitoes would rise up the wall the way the mosquitoes would do on summer nights during our long seaside holidays in Fromentine. I wondered if birds, black crows, drawn by the darkness, were going to start circling the roof.

Now the facade of the house was divided into two sections. The bottom part was black—the shadows had reached the upper floor—but the top half still shone in the sun. High above, the sky was flooded with golden yellow light, intense and radiant, like the light that sometimes shimmers on the sea.

I thought about the sea, and I felt like leaving.

In the house across the way, a house set at a slight angle to the road, someone turned on a television, suddenly illuminating a window, and then another light came on in a kitchen, I think—I could see cabinets. It seemed that those house lights drove the night back to the road, while the sky above it—the vast sky of the suburbs—remained bright.

The arborvitaes surrounding my sister's garden had lost their shadows; they were reduced to their mere dimensions.

The late-season warmth must have attracted a great many people to the parks open to the public; the park guards had to start blowing their whistles to round up visitors. The parks closed late, because their summer schedules were still in force. Now the guards have electric cars that allow them to catch up with walkers who've gone too far astray, the ones who dawdle alongside paths, hoping they'll be able to dodge the rules. I thought about the crowds leaving the parks and public gardens at that very moment. Maybe most people draw out Sunday evenings for fear of seeing the day end, for fear of stirring up an antique sadness; maybe it's a sadness we all share, the sadness you feel when things close down, when they come to a stop. I told myself it was an old, profoundly human recollection, something inscribed in us, the memory of the terrible alarm that must have stabbed Eve's heart when the Angel showed her out the gates of Paradise, and especially when she realized that the banishment was forever.

Claire Marie came back with some fruit juice and two glasses.

The lawn mower stopped.

A heady smell of cut grass climbed over the hedge that separates my sister's property from her neighbor's house and garden; the neighbor must have emptied the bag of grass cuttings and spread them under the hedge before putting his tools away. He'd started to water his lawn; the leaves of the hedge were dripping; on the sidewalk, some teenagers on rollerblades glided past.

Mélanie was still playing the same piece.

My sister said, "Schumann's 'Carnaval'—that's what she's working on. When Mélanie leaves, I don't know what we're going to do with the piano. I don't play, and neither does Christian. The whole floor will be more or less closed up."

I suggested, "You could learn to play too. You could. Haven't you ever thought about taking up music?"

"Yes," she admitted. "I've thought about it occasionally."

"You have time. You could learn. If you start now, you'll surely get to where you can play two or three pieces—I think it takes only a few lessons before a beginner can play 'Für Elise.'"

I was getting quite carried away. I said, "Everything's possible."

"Do you think so?" my sister asked wistfully. "I'd love to, I'd really love to."

Seeing that the idea appealed to her, I kept on insisting. "Of course, everything's possible, it's never too late," I said (even though, in fact, I didn't believe a word of it). But that was just the way it was; the more I felt bogged down in the torpor of that late afternoon, the more I insisted. "At least try. What have you got to lose?"

All of a sudden, Mélanie appeared. She planted herself in front of her mother, dressed up and made up, and announced that she was going out.

"With whom?" my sister asked. "With Clément?"

"We're going to the movies. Clément's picked out a film for us, it's playing in the center of town. There's an eight o'clock showing. I'll come home right afterward, I promise."

As she was leaving, Mélanie called, "See you soon!" She closed the gate behind her and walked away down the sidewalk. She made no sound; she'd let her hair down, and she was wearing ballet flats that gave her a dancer's gait.

"What time is it?" I asked.

"Oh, stay," my sister said. "It's Sunday, after all! You've got time! Look, the weather's so lovely. You never come to see us. You don't come enough. I know, I know, it's because of Luc."

I didn't reply. A strained silence followed, as it does every time we talk about Luc, and then she started talking again. "A little while ago, before you came— before Mélanie sat down at the piano, in fact—I wasn't reading, I was straightening up things in the house. I had the radio on and I was folding some clothes. I wanted to go through them, now that we're back from vacation, and toss out what we don't need anymore. Even though no matter what I do, there's always disorder. I must have started around three o'clock, and the time flew by. Mélanie called Clément and they stayed on the phone a good while. Everything was calm in the house, and the street was deserted; it was the Sunday afternoon calm. They were playing old hit songs on the radio. One of them was 'Indian Summer.' You remember it?"

I started singing softly:

We'll go
Where you want when you want
And we'll love each other still

"In fact," my sister murmured without looking my way, "it made me think of someone. I had an … encounter, years ago, didn't I ever tell you? Something happened to me."

AN ENCOUNTER!

The word sounded bizarre, what with all the shadows. I stopped singing at once. I remembered Mama's frequent command: "Go see what your sister's up to."

Actually, in some respects, Claire Marie reminds me of the ducks you sometimes see, ducks that look as though they're gliding on the water without making any movement at all themselves, but under the surface, their feet are paddling like mad. There's something *trompe-l'oeil* about those ducks.

"A very curious story, it's true," my sister went on. "I didn't understand what was happening to me. I've never understood myself."

She shot me a glance and then turned toward the cedar in the middle of her yard. The evening darkness was growing thicker. The lines of the tree trunk still stood out against the background of vegetation, but you couldn't see the details of the branches anymore.

"Bear in mind," said Claire Marie, "in stories like this, there's never anything to understand. And they're not very interesting."

I DIDN'T REACT AT FIRST. I told myself that if I insisted, Claire Marie would stop talking. I knew her; she'd make some trifling remark, get up, and go to turn on the exterior light, and then mosquitoes would begin to rise up dreamily in the luminous beam, as they used to do in the old days in Fromentine, because of the heat, the darkness, the freshly watered lawn. We'd sit there in silence and watch them; and once again, the chance would pass. The chance for me to figure out what was going on with my sister.

———

But she didn't get up. She didn't turn on the light. She seemed lost in her reverie, and her eyes stayed fixed on the tree.

I thought that our memories were like that cedar, that they had a solid trunk hidden in shadow. At night, when you lean out and look at the garden, you think everything's pitch black, but that's wrong. There, in the heart of the shadows, are those solid trunks. And if you walked in the dark without paying sufficient attention, you'd bang your forehead and give yourself a terrible bruise.

I asked, "Someone you still see?"

"Oh, no, certainly not! It's been over for a long time. As I said, it simply came back to me. On Sundays— don't you think?—certain things come back to you more than on other days."

She raised her too-thin arms, her bony elbows; she pulled her hair back and tried to fix it; she said, "On Sundays, you think about life."

And yet her story began in the most banal way. She'd filled in as a secretary in her husband's medical practice one afternoon. That day, she'd noticed a patient in the waiting room. Was it because he appeared to be more silent than the others? Or because it was rare to see male patients at that hour? In the dead center of the afternoon, when a small, temporary community made up of elderly people, children, and mothers fills doctors' offices, there he was in their midst.

As always, there was a kind of agitation in the waiting room. Women would come in, sit down, take off their children's jackets or push back their hoods to expose their faces, help them blow their noses, break out some cookies for them, speak to them softly, tell them stories. Or they'd page through magazines, as though at the hair salon, move around, ask the whereabouts of the rest room, and my sister would direct them with a discreet gesture and a smile.

The man didn't move. There was something massive about him, something silent, almost austere. His dark hair was straight, fairly long, brushed back, and he sat perfectly still, with his hands resting on his knees. Only once did he get up and approach the desk to verify the time of his appointment.

"You won't have long to wait," said Claire Marie. "The doctor's running just a little late."

He simply nodded and sat back down. Every now and then (she noticed), he looked at her.

Christian opened the door. My sister checked the appointment register and called out, "Monsieur Hermann?"

The man stood up, thanked her. After he went into the consultation room, she examined his entry in the register: Marc Hermann, 4:00.

When he came out to settle his bill, he lingered in front of her desk for a while, took out his cards, paid in cash, met her eyes again, and asked in an accent she couldn't identify, "Are you the secretary?"

"No," she said. "I'm filling in for her. I'm the doctor's wife."

The evening was very mild when she left the medical office. Christian had gone ahead—he had a few house calls to make. A damp smell rose from the vegetation in the gardens. It was in September, she tells me, more or less like now, just a little later.

Mélanie had brought several friends home with her. The living room was filled with little girls playing with their Barbies.

"They were at that age," my sister said. "Five or six years old. It's strange, I have a clear memory of that evening; I can see myself returning to the house, and all those little girls are there, squatting down and manipulating their dolls; I went and sat in the kitchen; I could hear them playing 'ladies.' After that, they wanted to watch some cartoons; they adored a cat who had problems with a bird or a mouse. You know the cat I mean," she said. "I can't remember its name...I think it was around even when we were kids. Didn't we watch a cat too, one that hopped around on two legs, as elastic as a piece of chewing gum? It was always chasing after the same bird or the same mouse, and it would get tied up by its own tail or catch its paw in a door. Remember?"

I pointed out that most cartoons have cats in them.

"That's true," my sister acknowledged.

I took a few sips of my juice; I too thought about the presence of little girls in a house, with their scratchy woolen leggings, their tangled hair, their way of kneeling on a chair next to a radiator, of staying there for hours, noses pressed against the windowpane, and what they're waiting for, what they're looking at, not readily apparent. They like cartoon cats, they make them laugh, because they naturally identify with the mice, which are weaker, but ten times smarter:

Can't-catch-me!
Can't-catch-me!
I'm too clever and you
can't-catch-me!

My sister went on: "That night, after Christian came home and I was putting Mélanie to bed, she asked me to tell her the story of the Little Mermaid.

"It was very warm in the room, and I was in no mood for storytelling. I remember that Mélanie's cheeks were damp. The piece of flannelette she was playing with, twisting it under her nose and over her chin, had a floral pattern; I recognized the fabric as what was left of one of my nightgowns.

"I recall that when I said, 'In the end, the Little Mermaid returns to play with her sisters in the immense Kingdom of the Sea,' when I pronounced the word 'Kingdom,' I saw an image of the sea in summer under the eight o'clock sun. I felt like leaving there and then.

"It lasted only a brief moment, because after I kissed Mélanie, as I was closing her bedroom door, I told myself I was lying to her, because the Little Mermaid dies. *What ideas*, I thought, *what ideas we put in their heads. They're only children! Those wounds! Those knives! Even fairy tales are too hard. Everything's too hard.*"

Maybe a month later, as Claire Marie was walking home after running some errands, a car pulled up alongside her. The driver lowered the window, and when she bent down, she was surprised to discover the man she'd seen once at her husband's office; she recognized his slight accent, which he corrected with very careful articulation. He smiled and said, "We've met before, I think. Aren't you the doctor's wife? Can I drop you somewhere? You've got a heavy load."

"*What would you have done* in my place?" my sister asked.

I thought about it; I said, "I wasn't in your place, but it sure was a funny coincidence. In any case, if you really were weighed down, it was very nice of him to offer you a ride, and very understandable too. Besides, he was one of your husband's patients."

"Exactly my reasoning," said my sister. "I accepted."

I couldn't make out her face very well. Around us in the garden, the trees and the hedge were gray, as though molded in the thick dough of the twilight. Only black holes marked the places where the windows on the upper floor were located (Mélanie had left hers open when she went out). From that moment on, my sister talked as if she'd forgotten my presence, without stopping, without looking at me, speaking in a monotone. The streetlamp opposite the house projected a steady illumination that elongated our shadows on the lawn; I could detect peaceful sounds I wasn't used to, because the empty yards, isolated from one another by walls and manicured hedges, were abundantly sonorous: you could hear discreet, well-bred traces of people's lives, their discernible imprint, the crunching of tires on the gravel of a driveway when a vehicle entered a gate, doors being shut here and there, calls, the sounds of television programs. Of course, a few little things were known about the neighbors: where they took their vacations, what schools their children attended. Claire Marie had told me that a fairly well-known painter lived in the neighborhood; she'd shown me his house, the glass windows of the big studio just above treetop level, but that was all. Every home held its mystery. In the evenings, figures would appear in kitchen windows; hands would pull net curtains closed or turn cranks to lower blinds, and reference points would vanish; windows, rectangles of light, would go dark, merging with the night.

I thought about secure fences, about intercoms with surveillance systems, about security cameras that allow the owner to monitor the street, to see who's ringing the doorbell outside the gate, to inhibit the unexpected. But you can't thwart everything, not every chance event, not every possibility.

On the evening she was telling me about in her serious, monotone voice, nobody had noticed anything, no one had observed the car that stopped at the curb for two or three minutes (the time it took the man to lower his window, the time it took my sister to decide) before melting into the moderate, smoothly flowing traffic on the avenue. There's always a bit of play, a gap or two, in space and time. Blind spots.

———

THE CAR WAS NO RECENT MODEL; the radio was tuned to a music station. The man drove for a moment without saying anything; then he switched off the radio and turned to Claire Marie: "May I invite you to join me for a drink? Just before I drop you off."

Inside the café, after a few banal remarks about the weather and Ville-d'Avray, he introduced himself: he was in import-export; his firm did business mostly with Latin America.

"What do you export?" Claire Marie asked politely.

"Specialized equipment for industry. I'm not going to bore you with that."

The café was brightly lit. For the second time, she was face-to-face with him, and she saw him in the light; she understood what had struck her about him; he had a broad forehead, and there was more gray in his hair than she'd thought; he was well past his first youth, in spite of his assured appearance; she even found that he looked a bit tired; he smoothed back his hair, and she registered his high cheekbones, his dark eyes—was he German? Argentine? His name was German, but after the war, hadn't some Germans emigrated and settled in South America? The hand he'd placed on the table, holding

43

the stem of his wineglass, was blunt, powerful, almost thick. She tried to identify his accent.

He was observing her closely, never turning away his eyes.

He talked to her about the ports and train stations he had frequented in Latin America and elsewhere, in his "other life." That was where he'd started; riding on trains that ran in the mountainous regions; it gave you the feeling that you wouldn't ever arrive anywhere, he said, it was an adventure, and he'd "knocked around" a lot before he finally succeeded. "I've almost killed myself several times," he said, "in my other life. Everybody has several lives, did you know that? But over there, business gets done quickly. You do business fast in dangerous countries, you have to take risks; I took a few back then; I wanted to succeed. There was no choice for me; I had to pull it off."

Not understanding much, my sister asked, "And you did succeed?"

He didn't answer. He took a pack of cigarettes out of his pocket, gave my sister a questioning look, suppressed his urge, and covered the pack with one thick hand. Then he smiled at her and said, in his careful articulation, "I succeeded in at least one thing, but before that: I got out of Hungary. I'm Hungarian, from Budapest."

He'd left his country when he was young because of the oppression, because of communism. Because of the closed horizons. Because of the barbed wire on the borders. Because of the watchtowers. He explained, "I got out in 1980. It was risky. Some people got shot at when they were spotted. Some didn't make it. Others succeeded. I succeeded. I took the risk. One day," he said, "I'll tell you about it. I didn't have much to lose. My father was a member of the opposition, and he was liquidated in the crackdown in 1956, when I was eight. My mother and my brother stayed on the communist side. I was the only one who left. I chose foreign lands. Exile."

My sister nodded vaguely, because those words (the 1956 crackdown, communism) referred to things that were vague to her; they were words connected with our childhood, images like archival records that didn't seem to apply to the actual world, but rather to a black-and-white past—as seen in films—and which, because of that, appeared as distant as the war. Like certain other words: the "Cold War"; the "Soviet bloc." She remembered: Hungary was part of the Soviet bloc. One got the impression that it was a sort of solid block, as massive as a building, whereas in fact it covered a vast territory shaded on maps—the "Eastern European countries," the ones behind the "Iron Curtain." She remembered having seen documentaries about revolutions with bizarre names ("the Velvet Revolution"); "the Prague Spring" crossed her mind; she recalled images of protest demonstrations, of dense crowds marching in the streets and confronting tanks, of men carrying banners. Did they all have, as Marc Hermann did, an energetic face, a dimpled chin, a barely perceptible, slightly mocking smile?

"*I'm boring you,*" he said, "telling you all that."

"Not at all," my sister said.

"I got married in France," he disclosed. "My wife's French."

My sister, embarrassed, bowed her head.

He watched her, still smiling, and tossed back his stiff hair.

"*How did you manage* to get across?" she asked. "Over the border, I mean. When you left."

"I did what everybody who got out did. At the time I'm talking about, things had already loosened up. You could travel a bit, but you had to leave your passport. I elected to cross over illegally. At night, when the guards were tired, just before dawn. After the winter. Not a very original plan. The worst part were the dogs in the villages; they'd get a whiff of you, and once they started barking, they never stopped. Do you want something else? I could use another glass of wine."

She refused and thanked him. "I have to go home."

"Then may I drop you off?"

They went back to his car, chatting as they walked, and after a detour found themselves pleasantly strolling the streets in the vicinity of the Chaville train station.

"Let's just say goodbye here," my sister said, all of a sudden. "It's much simpler. You needn't trouble yourself. It's late, and mine is the very next stop. I'll take the train."

But Marc Hermann didn't look like a man in a hurry. He protested: "But why? Don't go yet."

She stayed. She wondered how she'd be able to get away from him. Would she have to thrust out her hand?

Night had fallen. He'd lit a cigarette, and he was walking very close to her in the darkness, on her left side, closer than necessary. She moved away, but he drew nearer; she noticed his shuffling gait, as if he were dragging his shoes along the ground. He said, "Your husband advised me to stop smoking, but I'm not following that piece of advice. And not the other one he might want to give me either. I'm happy to have had this chance to see you again, you know."

She didn't answer.

He agreed to leave her at the station but then accompanied her downstairs to the platform. He considered her for a moment in the darkness. "I'll leave you now, I don't want to pester 'the doctor's wife.' Go on, you're going to miss your train."

He handed her his card: "If by chance you want to get hold of me someday. Get hold of me personally. Maybe you'll feel like doing that, you never know. That's my office number, my private line at my company. Call me. Don't hesitate."

She took the card and got on the train. While the train was moving away, she saw him moving away too, dragging his feet, and she smiled silently at herself, reflected in the window.

BACK HOME, my sister reread the card several times: MARC HERMANN—IMPORT-EXPORT. There was also a telephone number, and an address in Versailles. She hesitated to write the information in her address book and ended up leaving the card in the pocket of her raincoat, which she hung in the closet.

"I wonder," she said to Christian, "if you remember a patient who came to see you the day I filled in for your secretary, a few weeks ago? A man named Hermann."

"Maybe," said Christian. "Why?"

"I don't know. For no reason. The name came back to me. It's a foreign name."

"I see so many patients. Why should I remember that one?"

She wanted to ask, "What did he have?" But it would have been a waste of time.

In the course of the following days, she thought a little about Marc Hermann.

Then she thought about him less.

A damp autumn set in. You have to know what autumn's like in Ville-d'Avray. October. November. In the hundreds of terraced gardens that rose in tiers up the slopes of the hills, the plants were turning brown, the trees were shedding their leaves. The rain started in the morning, stopped around noon, and resumed toward evening. The neighborhood seemed dead, the gardens perpetually darkened by the showers; the slate roofs glistened; the sodden leaves macerated in heaps. As soon as night fell, the wet asphalt reflected extensive yellow crowns of yet unfallen leaves. The same ruined, melancholy prospect was reproduced on every street, one by one. People went out less.

Often, during her habitual promenade in the Parc de Saint-Cloud, my sister found herself alone on the pathways. She'd walk fast, thrusting her hands in her pockets. Her ankle boots trod on broad, damp, slippery leaves, still red and freshly fallen, that covered older, decomposed layers, some of them dating from the previous winter. Because the trees in the park were veterans planted long ago, they held up better. Their fall foliage, with the shiny red, the buttercup yellow, the brilliant russet of certain varieties—exactly the same color as the dried stems of the chrysanthemums people would leave in pots in cemeteries or decorate crossroads with—made patches of fantastic light when the shadows were settling in.

On her way home from her walks, when she was passing the rows of houses, a dog would bark. Invisible behind a fence or inside a garage, the dog would then emit a long, slow whine heavy with furious violence. It must have been running from one side to the other of the sliding door, trying to find a way out. Sometimes the story Marc Hermann had told Claire Marie—about the dogs in the villages on the Soviet side of the Hungarian border—would cross her mind. She had perused some books. She'd looked up the names of towns. She'd read that the border guards would shoot at people attempting to get across. Had anyone shot at him? He'd talked of a dangerous life. The boundary lines were electrified. There was no place to hide on the open plain.

Some people, once detected, would start running hopelessly, not stopping when the guards commanded them to halt and trained their weapons on them. Hermann had told her he'd crossed over before dawn.

She'd imagine that the border cut through woods, through large expanses of dismal pastureland, constantly frozen in winter, through silent, somnolent villages; she'd think about the barking of the hostile, confined dogs.

She'd go to pick up Mélanie.

When they came out of the school, the children would chase one another, bounding along the sidewalks. The more the day declined, the more the light seemed to irradiate the leaves; it flared up inside the streetlamps, turned very yellow, and faded away in the damp, dark shadows.

Claire Marie noticed that, without thinking, she was going more and more often to the window and looking out, the way she'd done when she was little. All night long on the border (so he'd told her), searchlights would illuminate the barbed-wire fences and the watchtowers; and when she looked out at her street, those luminous circles and those pockets of darkness were what she'd see, as they'd been seen in former times by people desperate to leave, to change their lives.

"You're not looking very well," Christian pointed out. "I'm going to prescribe you some vitamins."

What she didn't tell Christian (but confessed to me in her account) was that one day, while on her usual promenade in the Parc de Saint-Cloud, she'd had the feeling she was being followed. The pathway she'd taken skirted a broad, rectangular lawn, one of those where picnicking was authorized during the warmer months. The changeover from summer to winter time had just passed. The park was empty, the light faint—going but not yet gone—and the sensation of early nightfall was heightened by a cloudy, overcast sky, a sky full of rain. A few meters behind her, she heard, at regular intervals, the sound of footsteps. At first she thought she was imagining the sound, but then it continued. She walked the path beside the lawn all the way to the end, without turning around, as if she hadn't noticed anything; however, she kept a firm grasp on her umbrella. With relief, she spotted a couple to her right, began heading toward them, found a stairway, and went down, carefully monitoring the sounds behind her; they were scarcely more resonant on the stone steps.

A weak rain was falling. As she descended the steps, which led to another, lower path, she recognized the row of boxwoods running alongside it, pruned in the shape of little obelisks. This showed that she was approaching a more landscaped area of the park, near an exit; there was a fountain. She could make out several stone torsos, silhouetted against the darkness, as well as some statues in a circle—some kind of arbor, probably. The rain was falling into a central basin; a film of orange light (its source the streetlamps lining a road on the edge of the park) glimmered on the water.

The sound of footsteps had ceased, replaced by the shivering, continuous sound of the gently falling rain.

She stopped. There were several people around the pool. She approached them; she couldn't say whether one of them, a man leaning over the basin's stone rim, was the one who'd followed her. The rain was still pattering on her umbrella, as on a tambourine. She said to herself, *I must have been dreaming.*

Because of the damp weather, the seasonal flu epidemic started early that year. Many calls for Christian were transferred to their home phone; it rang incessantly, and every time she picked it up, my sister had to admit, she was vaguely expecting something.

One Wednesday in mid-December, Mélanie went off to visit her grandparents, who had been clamoring for her. Christian was at his office. Claire Marie stayed home alone.

The weather—the cold, dry, gleaming weather that accompanies the first freezes—had turned very beautiful. The neighborhood smelled of fire, because people were taking advantage of the dry days and burning piles of leaves.

Christian called right after lunch. "The waiting room is full, I'll be busy all afternoon, and then I'll have some house calls to make before I come home."

Claire Marie received the news cheerfully: "Don't worry, I have enough to keep me busy. I'm going to rake up the leaves."

But Christian may have been struck by something in her voice, because he didn't hang up at once. "Are you sure it's all right?" he asked. "When I'm finally through tonight, we can go out for dinner. Let's go to the Oasis in Saint-Cloud—it'll be a change for you. We'll let Mélanie stay with my mother and have ourselves a little evening. What do you say?"

"Why not?" said my sister.

"Have you noticed?" Christian added. "Our camellias have buds."

"Yes," said my sister.

She hung up, looked out at the garden, and observed the little green buds against the wall, hard as young

tomatoes. While she stood at the window and considered the camellias, saw how ready they were to burst into bloom, a terrible sorrow took hold of her, a heartache that prevented her from moving, that made its way to her across time, that seemed to come from very far away, from the empty hours of her childhood, from the waiting that had never ended. It took her breath away, so much so that she couldn't breathe.

She shook herself, opened the garage, groped around for a bit, looked for the rake but didn't find it, got annoyed, finally disengaged it from a jumble of tools, and began half-heartedly to rake up the last leaves on the lawn. Then she decided to call and find out how Mélanie's stay with her grandmother was going, but nobody answered; Mélanie and her grandmother must have gone out for a walk.

Claire Marie hung up the phone, felt the hollow ache in her chest again, and then, acting under an impulse, went to her closet, sought out the card in her raincoat pocket, turned the card over and over in her fingers for a long moment, returned to the telephone, and dialed Marc Hermann's number. The phone rang for a long time. She had the impression that it was ringing at the

end of long corridors. Her fingers were trembling. She hung up, but then the ringing began again, this time in her own house.

She recognized Marc Hermann's low-pitched voice: "Did you just call me? Who is this?"

"The doctor's wife," Claire Marie stammered. "Do you remember? You suggested that I—"

"But of course. Of course I remember. I wouldn't have dared to hope that you'd call me of your own accord. You're in luck. I had to go away on business at the beginning of the week, and I just came home yesterday. My plane was very late. Are you free right now, by any chance? I don't have any appointments at the moment. Would you like to meet somewhere? Shall I pick you up in my car? I can get to Ville-d'Avray quickly. Have you got a pen? I can come right away."

She demurred, but he insisted; he gave her the name of a street. He said, "It'll take me five minutes."

The car was waiting at the intersection; he got out and opened the door for her.

He was wearing a black pullover and a dark coat. "Where shall we go?" he asked. "Do you want to go to the Ponds? That's always pleasant."

And he started the engine.

My sister interrupted herself. "Do you go to the Ponds very often?"

"I've been there mostly with you and Christian."

I recalled that we would end our afternoon visits there. Christian wasn't fond of calmly loitering on the park lawn for any length of time, and so he'd suggest "a walk to the Ponds": "Are you two up for that? Shall we get off our butts?"

We'd do a tour of the Ponds. From wherever we were, we could follow the progress of the other walkers by watching the reflections of their heads and shoulders, upside down in the dark water.

———

Actually, I'd known those little lakes for a long time, I knew them *before I ever saw them*, because of some paintings by Corot that illustrated selections from the poetry and prose of Gérard de Nerval in our high school literature textbook.

I could practically see my sister strolling with her stranger in a setting composed of reflections, of beautiful trees, of leaves speckled with tiny light-colored patches, like eye floaters, as if the blurriness of dreams interposed itself between the image and the beholder (which is always the case with Corot).

I could practically hear, behind my sister's tale, the verses from Nerval's poem "El Desdichado" that appeared on the facing page:

I am the Somber Man, the Widower, the Unconsoled,
The Aquitainian Prince, he of the ruined tower.

When she sat in the car next to Marc Hermann, my sister said, "I just called you up, just like that"—embarrassed, awkward, but sheltering behind a lighthearted tone—"by chance." She lied: "I came across your card in my coat pocket. It gave me the opportunity. I had really thought I'd lost it."

"Chance doesn't exist, not completely," he said with a smile. "We can give chance a helping hand. We have freedom of choice."

She was silent.

As soon as they got out of the car, he lit a cigarette. He smoked while he walked, didn't talk much, and, as usual, dragged his feet (he had a strange gait); inhaling a smell she wasn't used to, the smell of tobacco, Claire Marie could feel the beginnings of regret for that impetuous telephone call.

They slowly walked around one of the ponds. The sun was luminous but very pale, almost white, and gave no warmth. It was four o'clock in the afternoon. Thin plates of ice floated here and there on the dark, muddy water, which seemed to contain a submerged forest of sunken tree trunks. If you leaned over, you could see a strange, gnarled, mangrove-like tangle of roots and reflections. Ducks floated among the reeds.

"Really, I feel bad," my sister resumed. "You have work to do. I'm sure I've disturbed you. But I've been wondering about you, and I have questions. The things you told me about Hungary..."

———

It was clear, however, that she wasn't fooling him, and that her pretexts sounded false.

It was also evident that she was getting herself enmeshed in an affair with someone she knew practically nothing about: a Hungarian, no longer very young, who came from "behind the Iron Curtain," who gave himself a certificate of heroism, acquired at a discount, for his escape (even though the Iron Curtain had ceased to exist a long time ago, even though the Iron Curtain was no longer anything but a memory). An "entrepreneur" involved in exports to Latin America, a job description that could, if you thought about it a little, cover a whole spectrum of shady activities. Basically, though, he was the one who was at hand. The "Somber Man," reporting for duty.

Maybe that was the meeting she'd had in mind the day she asked me if I didn't hope for "something else" from life.

I tried to remember—when was that? The dates ought to correspond. Back then, she hadn't said anything more on the subject. That was my fault: I'd dismissed her question. But the more I thought about it, the surer I was: it must have been precisely around that time when, under the pretext of an interest in Hungary, she threw herself into Marc Hermann's arms, out of idleness and boredom, because she was hoping for *something else*, like a bee buzzing against a windowpane.

He saw her coming. My sister was easy prey (even if I express my reasoning stupidly). All he'd had to do was to look at her in a certain way, to declare himself to her very frankly—*You attract me*—and to ask insistent questions: *Do I shock you? Do I make you blush?* Or to suggest, with a smile, *Suppose I try my luck.* All he'd had to do was to say, *Perhaps you want it too.* Anyone who saw my sister registered the impression she made of being anxious but available, her air of living "on the moor"— which I've privately called her Lady-with-a-Lapdog look, ever since I read Chekhov's short story.

I understood the mechanism so well! Her dismay when she felt she was trapped, under quarantine, in her house in Ville-d'Avray (as she admitted), when she realized that her life was running "on a track": Mélanie was growing up, Christian was focused on his patients and the smooth functioning of his practice; he loved her in a routine, comfortable, absentminded way. What hopes, what expectations remained to her? What could still happen? Would the passing hours simply "wound" her, one by one? There it was, an old quotation that came back to me out of nowhere, or at least from very far away, a Latin riddle Monsieur Jumeau had translated for us from an inscription on a Roman sundial: *They all wound; the last one kills.* It meant the hours, he explained. Child that I was, this image of wounding made a strong impression on me. At the time, I didn't imagine that a wound could be purely internal. Or, to be more exact, I didn't see time as a wound.

I said to myself, *Nevertheless, it's true; nevertheless, it's right; ultimately, that's just what they do, the hours, and they even do it so fast!*

Hermann had surely been joking, trying to make her laugh. My sister's a rather serious person, but when she laughs, her shyness—a reserve some may take for coldness—disappears; at first, she laughs as though incredulously, but then openly, with artless spontaneity.

I felt anger toward that man. Because he took advantage of the situation; because he understood nothing about my sister.

For him, it was just a matter of curiosity, a way of seeing how she laughed, of seeing what kind of reaction to a few facile little provocations he could elicit from a shy woman, a truly "dreamy" woman, a woman of Ville-d'Avray.

"I LIVE ON THE OTHER SIDE," he told her, "over there." He made a vague gesture toward the thick mass of the forest. "We're practically neighbors. Speaking of which, I saw you once or twice in Saint-Cloud with your daughter. You do have a daughter, don't you?"

"In Saint-Cloud?" my sister asked.

"Yes, in Saint-Cloud. I spotted you in the park. I go there now and then. There was a time when I used to walk there with my wife."

"'Spotted'?"

"Recognized, if you prefer. Forgive me, I haven't mastered all the nuances of your language. You're often alone. Afterward," he said negligently, "I may as well be sincere, I found your residence; it's not hard to find"—he laughed a little—"*the doctor's wife*. While I was out walking in the evening, I passed your home several times. It's a lovely house. I suppose your rooms are the ones that look out on the garden."

She'd picked up some twigs and was breaking them into little pieces while listening to him with great interest, concerned by the images his revelations aroused in her, as well as by the words he'd pronounced with a curious insistence and a kind of jubilation in his voice: "the doctor's wife."

"Don't torture those poor twigs," he said. "They haven't done you anything. You're so nervous! I can even tell you that during your walks, you wore a light-colored raincoat, beige or ochre. You often had it on early in the fall."

"You mustn't think," said my sister, nearly speechless. "You can't possibly think."

"In that case, why did you call me? I know women are illogical, but even so."

He leaned forward, took her hands, and pried open her fists so that she dropped the twigs.

My sister protested weakly: "I have to go home now, I really have to go home. They'll be waiting for me."

"But why? What's your hurry? Just this one time. Why don't you want to stay with me?"

"My garden," my sister wailed.

"Your garden can wait. I find you distant today.

You were much more spontaneous that other time, in the café. I was sorry. I had to travel early the next morning—my flight left at seven. I almost called you from the taxi. I even almost called you from abroad. I'd found your telephone number."

"You shouldn't have," said my sister, "you absolutely shouldn't have. Let's not talk about it anymore. It was ridiculous."

"Why was it ridiculous?"

"Because," said my sister, drawn through her own fault onto slippery ground. She fell silent.

"Why ridiculous?" he repeated, more affectionately this time, and tried to pull her toward him. Then he reassured her: "Don't be angry. I'm so sincerely happy to be in your company. There are too many people here, don't you think? Let's go find a quiet path."

They'd completed the loop. He made her cross a road and led her to the Fausses-Reposes[1] Forest. On

---

1 *Translator's Note:* The Forêt de Fausses-Reposes, a former royal hunting ground, now a national forest, lies partially in Ville-d'Avray and adjoins the Parc de Saint-Cloud. Its name—which literally means "False Rests"—is a hunting term for the ruses employed by animals that hide in a fold of ground or a thicket to escape hunters and their dogs. In English, one might say that such a quarry is "playing possum."

weekdays, nobody went there, except perhaps for a jogger trotting along and looking straight ahead, or an indifferent horseman on one of the sunken paths, under the forest cover. They got out of the horseman's way; he nodded politely to them and rode on, his body lurching a little askew on his beast's enormous hindquarters.

Marc Hermann let her pass in front of him when the path narrowed. He told her that he'd waited for her to call, that he hadn't thought she would, that he'd driven back to the intersection where he'd come upon her the first time, returning from her errands. He described the light-colored raincoat she'd worn early in the fall. He waited until they were some distance into the woods before he ventured to embrace her again.

Sunset came very soon. Since the weather was quite dry, the sky, visible through the bare branches, turned red as though irritated when the sun went down.

Do you know where the name *Fausses-Reposes* comes from?" my sister asked Christian while they were sitting at their table that evening, next to the Oasis's big window.

"I think there's been a change in the spelling," Christian said. "I think it may have started out as *Fosses²* *Reposes*. I'd have to check; it must refer to some episode in the past, I don't know which. Something in the war. Maybe some Resistance fighters were executed. There were certainly Resistance groups operating in these parts. If they got caught, they were put in front of firing squads right away."

---

2 *Translator's Note*: As used here, *fosses* means "pits" or "graves."

But when he saw her worried look, he corrected himself: "The name's probably very old. The war I'm talking about may have taken place long ago, like the Hundred Years' War. Or maybe a legendary war. Many place-names are connected to old legends or superstitions. There's nothing real in any of that. It was just a dark, scary forest. Dark forests have always scared people. And then there's the Ponds, very nearby. And extremely deep, remember. Maybe they were the original *fosses*."

He tried to reassure her, but the more he played down her worries, the more he talked about old, unfounded legends and about the calm suggested by the name *Fausses-Reposes*, the more she was convinced that something terrible, something excruciating, must have happened in that forest. She began to think about one of those news stories that the papers feature for a week and then forget, stories that remain shut up in the damp darkness, in the creaking of the tree trunks when they move, in the vague fear of those who remember the reports and who say, *Didn't something happen here? Wasn't someone terribly . . . imprudent?*

"Wasn't it there," she asked, "that they found some politician? Drowned in a few meters of water? It reminds me of something I read. A politician drowned in a pond."

"I don't know," said Christian. "I don't remember, and nobody cares. In any case, they concluded it was suicide. When politicians are involved, they always conclude it was suicide."

Her cheeks were red, her look vacant; she thought that the way she'd spent her afternoon could be read in her eyes as in a book. She avoided looking directly at him and sat turned toward the Parc de Saint-Cloud, which lay drowned by the night.

I forgot to clarify something," my sister went on.

"At that particular moment in Ville-d'Avray, there was a scare that everyone blew out of proportion, which is what happens in towns like ours. You understand; everything's so little here, and so peaceful. A suspicious man was reported in the vicinity of the train station. He'd been seen several times on what's called the 'trail,' a kind of path, very steep, that follows the railroad tracks, passes over them on the viaduct above the tunnel, and allows pedestrians to reach Sèvres. The trail's often deserted in the afternoon. Some people take it when they've just got off trains, or some, mostly children and solitary women, use it as a shortcut or make it part of their walks. When you're up there, because

72

of the viaduct, the way the trains plunge into the tunnel, and all the weeds, you feel a little like you're in the mountains."

An informational meeting was held at the school. The administration took the eyewitness accounts seriously. The children were bringing home warning notices that had been slipped inside their schoolbags. They all said the same thing: that the man in question had been "observed" several times, that his description might correspond to that of a wanted individual—photocopies of various composite sketches were also given out—and that though there was no cause to panic, people should be vigilant: the proximity of the train station gave reason to think that the man traveled on the Saint-Lazare–Versailles Rive Droite line. He couldn't be accused of very much: he'd hang around on the trail, shaded by a tree, and when little girls came up the path he'd ask them, *What's your name?* Some children said they'd also seen him on the viaduct, leaning over the parapet to watch the trains pass and observe the travelers' movements from above. Maybe he was simply a man who had nothing to do.

"Naturally," my sister said, "I asked Mélanie about it. I said, have you seen this gentleman? If you see him, you tell me. Don't answer him and start walking fast; you must never speak to a stranger."

I smiled and said, "You could have taken that advice yourself."

She didn't reply.

IT RAINED ALL MORNING the day after the walk to the Ponds.

It was still raining in the middle of the afternoon, at the deadest hour of the day, when someone rang the bell at the gate. Claire Marie was dealing with some overdue invoices; she jumped; the children were in school, the street empty. She waited a minute, then got up without making any noise, went to the window, looked through the curtains. It was only a neighbor of hers, Madame Dufaux, a small, gray-haired woman who lived near the station. She looked breathless and drenched, and she was shaking her umbrella.

"Excuse me for disturbing you, Claire Marie, but I'm so worried. And out of breath, as you see. I walked very fast, the street goes uphill to your house, and I'm starting to find inclines difficult. I wanted to warn you that I saw a police van in front of a house in the neighborhood.

It was parked, but they'd left the flashing lights on. I don't know what they were doing. They stayed there a good while, maybe as long as two hours, according to the neighbors—around noon, they said. I wonder if they were there to arrest someone. And just now there was a strange-looking guy in front of the café. It's not the first time I've seen him. The other times, he was hanging around outside the train station. Could he be the one they're talking about in the newspaper? The one who loiters near the viaduct? I came to warn you as fast as I could. I figured you were home. Don't you want to make a phone call? If it's him, we should notify the police."

She talked fast, panting all the while: "It's dark in your living room! You don't turn on the lights? I turn mine on at three o'clock now! The days have become so short! It's awful!"

Claire Marie offered her guest some tea, turned on the lights, and went to look for the warning notice the teachers had slipped into Mélanie's schoolbag.

They sat in the living room and bent over the notice: a simple photograph, no doubt a photocopy of a photocopy (as you could tell by looking at it). The ink was smudged on the lower part of the faces of three men, photographed head-on: all had very close-cropped, almost shaved hair; for a moment, my sister felt a kind of fear; she understood what she'd been dreading. *It isn't possible*, she thought. *They're much younger. Don't be stupid.*

And she reassured herself: *He's the head of a company. He runs a business. He has an office, a "storefront."*

Madame Dufaux also studied the photograph; she took out her glasses, examined it under the lampshade, seemed disappointed: "It's not him. I don't think it's him. It doesn't look like him; but as you see, it's hard to recognize anyone from this."

"Maybe the man you saw works in Ville-d'Avray— maybe in the station, at the café or in maintenance," Claire Marie suggested.

"He looked like he was mostly just hanging around, staring into houses, if you see what I mean. I stayed at my window and watched him at his little game. He went up and down the street several times. Doing what? It wasn't good weather for walking; rain was coming down, and it was quite chilly. I got drenched just coming here. Guys like that, I can spot them, he's not the first one I've seen. Some try different combinations on the outside keypads, looking for the right entry code. I stand at my window and keep them under surveillance. I can make out the ones who lurk around in cars. There are some like that, you know. Who notices when a car's been parked in the same spot too long? You have to keep an eye on everything! You can't ever be cautious enough. Have you seen what goes on in the U.S.?"

"America's far away," my sister said.

"I just assume that anything can happen here too. Did you know there was a burglary at the painter's house two weeks ago? They didn't publicize it very much, but I heard people talking about it at the bakery. They slipped into the house in the middle of the night. First they got into the garden without being detected by the alarm system. The most frightening part is that there was no break-in. They had the code, or the keys. They were very well informed, because the painter was away on a trip. All the neighbors were sound asleep; nobody heard a thing."

"Thanks, I didn't know that," my sister replied. "It was very nice of you to have gone to this trouble; I'll be careful, I promise."

She stood on the threshold and watched Madame Dufaux do battle with her umbrella, open it, and walk away under the streetlamp. Then Claire Marie closed and double-locked the door.

The garden and the street were black, it was still raining, and the big, modern hanging lamp in the ground floor office was reflected in the window in front of her, enkindling dots of light in the raindrops that landed on the other side of the panes with a small sound, the kind you could make with your fingertips, and then ran down toward the corners in long, winding streaks. The wind had come up, and now the rain started descending in torrents.

She went to the closet, felt in the pocket of her raincoat, found the card, and read it again: MARC HERMANN—IMPORT-EXPORT.

No connection, she thought. *It's a business like any other. Besides, I have his telephone number.*

But when she raised her head, she too said, "How dark it is! It's as though the raindrops want to come inside."

She had distant memories of a window left open, of rainwater turning the floor under a radiator gray: a summer storm of long ago, when it had been hot and muggy all day long, and then the rain had come all at once, and the windows had been left open—one of those very heavy rains that make an enormous noise, one of those that comfort and sadden.

She gazed at her own reflection in the window; then she suddenly thought, *I can be seen from outside.* She turned off the light, lifted the curtain, and for a long moment looked out at the dark street. Nothing moved. The parked cars remained in their places; she counted them and tried to discover whether there was anyone inside any of them. But why would anybody be in a car? Who would park on a residential street on a weekday afternoon in a pouring rain and stay in the car? At that time of day, people are at work. Then she thought (or rather remembered): *We can give chance a helping hand.*

The telephone rang.

She didn't answer; the house was silent, except for the hum of a machine and maybe, way down in the cellar, the more muffled, more regular sound of the furnace. She went up to Mélanie's room; the rain was louder there because it fell on the roof slates of the false attic.

Hidden by the curtain on Mélanie's window, she once again gazed out at the street, at the parked cars, which she counted again. In the distance, the neon lights of the station covered some wet roofs with an orange glaze (you could see a bit of the station, a tiny portion of the platform, from Mélanie's room). As she was turning away, her hand struck the piano keys, and the strings vibrated with such intensity that she trembled at the sound.

"What have I done?" she asked herself aloud. "What's happening to me?"

Nevertheless, when the rain eased off, she went out.

She walked up the trail and saw the man Madame Dufaux had been talking about. She knew it was him. He was standing by the enclosure wall of a house, under a tree that provided no shelter because it had no leaves.

He wore a thin anorak whose lining must have offered him little protection from the rain, which was not very hard but quite persistent; there were dark wet streaks on the wall behind him. At his feet she saw a bag, propped against the wall and probably containing a rolled-up duvet. She thought, *He sleeps there.* Farther up the trail, a cabin stood on an otherwise empty lot.

He was eating a piece of wet bread, which he hid when he saw her. The path is quite narrow and dark; it was hard for two people to meet on it and ignore each other. There was no sign that the man was begging, no container for coins; he asked for nothing; the rain had plastered his hair against his skull; he looked meager and chilled and so acutely uncomfortable, so filled with a hostile despair he didn't wish to show, that my sister was touched.

She looked in her change purse and held out a few coins to him. He looked away.

That evening, after tucking Mélanie in, she went to bed and read for a while. More accurately, she pretended to read, because it had become impossible for her to concentrate; instead of reading, she asked herself all sorts of bizarre questions. She wondered if her reading light was visible through the window, if the yellow point of the light shone between the shutters; she relived, in a continuous loop, her recent excursion to the Ponds.

She'd been so confused that she hadn't noticed when they left the signed walk near the road and briefly followed a forest trail, a straight path whose surface was covered with leaves. They'd walked in the opposite direction of the vehicles passing through the forest; she could hear them in the distance; the evening was advancing; she'd realized how late it was when she suddenly saw the black treetops silhouetted against the cold sky, which had the gray, watery color that precedes dusk. She'd said, "Take me back, I must get home now, right away."

He'd bowed and accompanied her to a point a couple of blocks from her house. She'd reached the Oasis very late.

She abruptly closed her book and said to Christian, "It seems there's been a burglary in the neighborhood."

"Yes," Christian said. "Pretty destructive. They broke into the painter's house at night. They had weapons. Guys who would stop at nothing, obviously—they took some big risks. They knew what they were going to find. Very well-informed crooks. They had certainly cased the place: they even had tools for cutting the canvases out of their frames. They must have spent days if not weeks checking out the house and laying their plans. For the time being, it would be a good idea to keep the doors locked."

Then she said, "A man's been hanging around the neighborhood lately."

"What man?" Christian asked.

"I don't know. Madame Dufaux came over to warn me. A tramp."

The telephone rang two or three days later, almost at the same hour—just as dusk was about to fall—as Madame Dufaux's visit. This time, Claire Marie answered the phone. Of course it was Hermann.

He seemed to hesitate. "I hope," he began, "you're not angry at me for my insistence the other day."

Then he gave it a try: he explained that he had a certain amount of leeway in his schedule, and that he could free up some time in the late afternoon or early evening on certain days. He could juggle his appointments. "I'd so much like to see you again," he said. "Would you by chance be free this evening, for example? Could you meet me this evening?"

"Yes," my sister said, without any very clear idea of what she was doing.

"In two hours? Perfect. It's perfect that you're available. Would Versailles be all right with you? That's where my office is. Could you come to Versailles? It would just be a quick train ride for you. It would be simpler." He gave her the name of a street. "Will you remember it? I'll park my car on the right, near the train station, past the taxis. There are always open parking spots; it's quite easy. I'll leave my lights on. See you soon?"

"Yes," said my sister.

I'm stunned by your behavior," I observed. "You recognize that you're starting to get scared, and you go ahead anyway. I have to say, for a busy man, he had a good deal of free time. For the head of a company who traveled a lot. That didn't surprise you? He had your telephone number. Which you never gave him. And then, he'd made sure to tell you about his wife . . . It doesn't add up, none of it."

"I know," she said. "As you can imagine, I've had plenty of time to reflect on all that. I myself don't understand what got into me. Let's just say it was 'beyond my control.'"

———

She stretched, leaning back on her chair, and sighed. "I'm not trying to justify myself." She confessed that on the following days, in spite of everything, she'd agreed to several meetings with Hermann, always on Thursdays, the days when Mélanie stayed at a neighbor's after school. It was the middle of the winter. Night came early, thus enhancing the discretion of her departures.

She'd walk down the dark shoulder of the street to the station at the hour when the offices empty out and the day, as they say, is behind you; the hour when suburbanites surge into the stations of the Transilien rail network; the hour when exhausted, inert passengers stand absentmindedly in the railroad cars, gliding along and watching the lights and station names slip past: Puteaux, Suresnes, Vaucresson, Marly-le-Roi, L'Étang-la-Ville.

The farther the train got from Paris, the blacker the darkness would become; the line went through entire neighborhoods whose dark streets, lower than the railroad tracks, were barely visible; nothing could be seen but the shapes of the windblown trees and bushes alongside the tracks, some small cafés, stores whose illuminated fronts succeeded one another in a blur of speed; these glimpses were interrupted only by the violent orange neon of the train stations' lights. Some stations, where the train didn't stop—it was a "direct"—passed by like movie sets.

At *the Versailles station,* the passengers would push through the ticket barriers en masse, leaving the platform as empty as a street after a storm. The concourse was drafty; once she caught a nasty chill and began to cough.

He'd be waiting for her near the station. She could identify his car because its lights were on; he'd be listening to music, often the same piece, or making a phone call; she'd tell herself he was attending to his business. He'd always end the call as soon as he saw her. One day, when he'd driven them to one of the park's dark entrances and was just in the act of parking, a car appeared at the gate. The vehicle's headlights illuminated the gate's gilded scrolls. It opened. An interior barrier rose; someone must have inserted a card into the security system. The car passed inside; its headlights made a long colonnade of trees emerge out of the night. Then the two opened wings of the gate returned to their former position.

They never entered the park, Claire Marie and Hermann. It was too late.

THE CAFÉS where he'd arrange to meet her were never the ones that tourists went to. He'd choose places with discreet terraces, places whose decor hadn't changed since the 1980s: cane-bottomed chairs, worn redleather banquettes, and faux-marble tables that facilitated intimate conversations. When he was late, she'd sit all the way at the back to wait for him. One or two guys would be gloomily sipping their espressos, others would be buying cigarettes, while groups of disoriented Japanese or Americans studied maps of the Palace of Versailles and its grounds, whose gates had just closed. When Versailles closes, it's as if the city's heart stops beating. All the streets run toward the somber mass of the royal estate.

SHE'D LOOK AT HER WATCH, on the alert for approaching headlights; pairs of them would pass in single file (because their brightness dazzled her, the face behind the steering wheel was never visible), she'd try to make him out—and later, she told me, years later, years and years, after they'd lost all contact, when she wasn't even sure she'd recognize him if she were to run into him

(it's almost fifteen years ago, she said, which is really crazy!),

it happened to her, it would still happen to her, at night, on side roads, every time a car would come upon her from the opposite direction, its headlights suddenly appearing, an invisible shape behind the wheel, the *possibility* suddenly appearing,

perhaps for a thousandth of a second, a quarter of a second,

time

always separating them, and indifference, no doubt, and incomprehension, she said,

this question would flash through her:

Is that you? Where are you?

HE'D ENTER THE CAFÉ with his slightly dragging, possibly exhausted step, thrusting his eternal pack of cigarettes into his pocket. He'd glance toward the leather banquettes, searching for her, squint to improve his chances of spotting her in her refuge, smile when he located her. Once or twice, seeing him from a distance like that, as he was pushing through the door of the café, at a moment when he didn't know he was being observed, she thought he looked strange; he always wore the same long, dark overcoat, always left it open; he gave an impression of strength and attrition. But she didn't know why, she could never explain it to herself, and yet when he took her hand and held it in his to warm it— saying, I'm so glad to see you, your hands are cold—or put it on his knee, she sensed that he felt for her, in spite of everything, an inexplicable tenderness.

She was almost sure that he was lying to her about a great many things, but she felt certain that he was alone and that his solitude was complete, so dense that she could perceive the space it occupied around him, and that solitude touched her heart.

He never talked about his present life, but always about his "life before," in Hungary, about his apartment building in the suburbs, about his brother, who was stagnating somewhere, and from whom he seldom heard. He told her, "We listened to a lot of music in my house, but I never took any lessons. We couldn't afford it. I'm not an intellectual. I was past thirty when I came over to the West, I didn't speak the language. In France, I did odd jobs, first in restaurants, then as a laborer on building sites. I pulled myself up by my bootstraps. I even spent time in prison, you know." He told her, "I trust you."

He was the reason why she made Mélanie take piano lessons. Christian didn't want to force her. Claire Marie insisted.

Once he said, "My wife doesn't know anything about my business. She doesn't know anything about anything at all." On another day, he made an admission: "Things between us aren't going very well. We've separated. We have too many differences, we're too far apart."

He'd drive her back in his car and stop a few blocks from her house, making sure she had enough time to pick up her daughter from the neighbor who was minding her; he'd look at his watch and say, "You have five minutes." She'd get out, and he'd roll along slowly beside her; she'd clench her teeth and walk on, her expression giving no hint that she saw him. She'd say to herself, *This is the last time, we're done.*

But he'd lower the window, stick his head out, smile at her, and say, "Thursday, same time?" Then he'd drive away.

In the car, he drove too fast. Once, as they were leaving Versailles, he ran a red light and they were pulled over by the police; she could see his anger, could sense that he had intended to mash the accelerator to the floor the moment the gendarme stepped out of his van, but he had controlled himself, probably because she was with him, and held out his driver's license.

"This is an old license," said the policeman. "It's foreign, you haven't kept it up to date, so it's not valid anymore. And as far as I can see, you haven't had the vehicle inspected either. Plus, you were driving too fast; at that speed, you could run over somebody, are you aware of that? You could kill someone on the spot."

The gendarme paused for a moment, turning the document over and over in his hand with a skeptical look on his face. He wrote down the number on the license plate.

"Are you a foreigner?"

"Naturalized French," Marc Hermann replied in a low voice.

The policeman nodded; he looked alternately at the car and at Hermann's austere, expressionless face, and then he tried to distinguish my sister's face through the driver's window. She remained mute the whole time.

"Are you Madame Hermann?" the gendarme asked.

"No," my sister said.

The gendarme asked no more questions. He walked around the car to place himself on the passenger's side and stared at my sister as though he were trying to memorize (and later to recall) her face. Was he liable to identify her? Had he ever been to her husband's office? If he wrote up a report, would he put "Monsieur Hermann and his passenger"? "Monsieur Hermann and an unidentified female"? "Monsieur Hermann and the doctor's wife"?

"Where are you going?"

"Ville-d'Avray," said Marc Hermann. "I'm in a hurry. I have an appointment."

In the end, the policeman let them go with a simple warning: Don't do it again. Obey the speed limits.

I interrupted Claire Marie: "Of course you realize he didn't have any appointment. He was lying. Lying came easily to him."

"I don't know," my sister said. "Accusing him is easy too. Anybody in his situation would have lied." Then she conceded, "It's possible. Maybe he lied about lots of things. What would that change?"

"Maybe he didn't have a wife at all. Maybe he had no business at all. You didn't know where he came from. From out of nowhere. Didn't any of that bother you?"

"Yes, it did," said my sister. "I had no idea where it was leading me. I told you that I found some of his behavior strange, but I was never really afraid. Or maybe just once, near the end."

THAT THURSDAY, a heavy, cold, disheartening rain inundated the landscape.

The rain streamed down the big glass windows of the Versailles train station and made seeing difficult, so much so that Claire Marie had trouble finding the car. He was talking on the telephone, softly, in Hungarian, and cut the connection as soon as she opened the door; she could feel that he was irritated. He drove off right away. "I can't go back home," he told her. "I'm having some problems, some big problems."

As always, he was driving too fast, and he sped through several red lights.

"What problems?" she asked.

But he simply replied, "Problems with suppliers. A ship with cargo in the harbor. I won't pay. They're threatening me. There are some guys in this business who'll stop at nothing."

They had left Versailles and entered a less populated area, an area my sister recognized, on the way to the Route Forestière du Cordon de Viroflay.

According to her, they drove along the same portion of the forest several times; it was terribly dark, awash in a deluge; Hermann kept driving without a word, randomly, consumed by a mute rage.

He braked in front of a store that was part of a gas station. "I have to stop," he said. "I forgot to pick up a few things."

Claire Marie watched him run through the downpour; she waited for him in the car, listening to the rain pounding on the roof and keeping an eye on her watch. Time passed, and he didn't return. *What could he be buying?* she wondered. *What's going on? Did he get out to make a phone call? Is he being followed?*

Cars with their headlights on filed past; she could barely see them through the fogged-up windows; the vehicles seemed to be fleeing, hurrying toward inhabited places; in the halos around the headlights, a thick curtain of raindrops was visible.

Finally he returned, his face expressionless; he opened the door roughly, threw some bags onto the back seat, and restarted the car.

She didn't dare speak.

She had a feeling he was going back to the forest.

He's been in prison, she thought. *For what?*

Suddenly, he flicked on his blinker and slowed down. On that part of the road, in the heart of the woods, there was a place, a hunting lodge or café, whose completely drenched terrace she could see; it was one of those former forester's houses transformed into a chalet, where hikers would stop for a midday break. There were no lights on; but maybe, my sister hoped, maybe there was someone inside in the dark, standing behind the counter, waiting for the unlikely arrival of some customers, looking out at the rain, suffused with the sadness of the rain and the forest. That was what she hoped, with all her heart. She felt she was lost.

He braked, stopped the car in front of the building, and switched off the engine, but he didn't open the door. And made no move to get out. The interior of the café looked deserted. Tables were stacked inside. In front of the door, a bucket caught the rain that was pouring down from a gutter without letup.

"Where are we?" my sister asked.

"I don't know," he said in a clipped voice. "As you can see, it's a forest house. We're stopping here."

She protested: "I'd rather go home."

"Five minutes. I'm thirsty, and it's dangerous to drive in such a storm."

"It's closed," said my sister. "This is pointless. There's nobody inside."

He pulled her to him and tried to kiss her, but she struggled and he let her go.

"I wish I understood," he sighed.

They remained for a while without speaking. Claire Marie, increasingly anxious, counted the minutes on the dashboard clock. He lowered the window on his side and smoked a cigarette. Rainwater came in through the opening.

———

"*I've had enough of these café meetings,*" he said at last, throwing away his cigarette. "I want you to come to my place. It's not the first time I'm asking you that. Why won't you come to me?"

"To your house?"

"Don't be stupid. To my office," he said. "In Versailles. My company's in Versailles. You have the address—I gave you my card. I'll wait for you there tomorrow. Your choice. If you don't come, I'll understand."

He started the car and didn't speak again for the rest of the trip.

The following day, when the time of their meeting approached, she went out. She couldn't sit still. My sister had always been incapable of choosing. She was also incapable of breaking off the relationship. She didn't ask herself whether she loved Marc Hermann. She was yielding little by little—I see that now, and something in me understood her—to the novel-like element he imported into her life. And natural curiosity also played a part. She was saying to herself, vaguely, *I'm going to see. I'm going to* know.

It was one of those peaceful cul-de-sacs, perpendicular to wide avenues, that are called *villas* in Paris. The low stone building, very ordinary-looking, stood on the left; on the right, the short, narrow, paved alley was bounded by the garden wall of a big house whose roof was all she could see. The hour wasn't very late, but standard time was still in force, and when she reached her destination, darkness shrouded the far end of the *villa*. My sister intuited rather than saw some trees, surely old veterans that had been part of the "royal domain" before its margins were divided into lots and gradually bitten off by the town. From its origins, the entire neighborhood retained something silent, old-fashioned, neglected, but also vaguely aristocratic. There was no plaque on the building indicating a company with Hermann's name. Or, to be more exact, there was only one plaque, affixed to the main entrance. It read: DR. ZHANG—MANUAL MANIPULATION, ACUPUNCTURE, and, at the bottom of the metal plate, SECOND FLOOR.

Claire Marie pressed the button that opened the door; she entered an unremarkable lobby and saw the metal bars of an elevator gate and a wooden staircase without a runner. She stopped and listened, unable to decide whether to call the elevator or climb the stairs or leave. She didn't turn on the timer that controlled the light.

More minutes passed, becoming a block of time, maybe a quarter of an hour; my sister's will weakened. The longer she stayed down there, the later she was; Marc Hermann must be growing impatient already, interpreting her failure to appear as definitive, walking up and down in his rooms, nervous and disappointed. She pictured the expressionless face she'd seen when the police had pulled them over. She was surprised that there was no plaque, no sign for clients announcing the name of the company. Was he there? The place was so silent! Before entering the building, she'd carefully noted another odd fact, namely that there was no light coming from any of the windows on the third floor (the one indicated on the card). Did his office face the back?

The silence was so complete that Claire Marie could hear the ticking of her watch, which was telling her, *Make up your mind, time is passing.* (She wondered: *Is the watch beating faster than my heart?*)

A light came on in the frosted glass of the entrance door—a dim, pale-yellow rectangle, like neon. She waited a few seconds, giving herself time to settle down, and then she stepped back outside and walked, hesitantly, to the corner of the building, at the end of the cul-de-sac. Looking up, she could see that the light was being projected from the second floor; probably from the window of the acupuncturist's office. Dr. Zhang was seeing a patient. In the dusty room overlooking the cul-de-sac, there must have been a guy lying on his back with various needles skillfully thrust into his knees and his thorax.

At the thought of the dusty little office, with diagrams pinned to the wall, cross-sectional images of the human body showing the points that transmit nerve impulses, my sister felt something give way in her.

Seized by panic, she ran toward the side alley, followed it in the direction of the Versailles city center, and walked for a long time, taking streets at random, suddenly feeling liberated, certain that it was all over.

AND HIGH TIME IT WAS. For when she went to pick up Mélanie that evening, the child's hand grew tense in hers.

"Papa asked me if you were picking me up after school."

"And what did you answer him?"

"I said you were coming less often," the little girl declared. "I said you were late a lot; I don't see you very much anymore."

They took a few steps together.

"What did your father say?" my sister said, resuming the conversation without looking at the girl.

"Nothing," the little one said, staring straight in front of her. Then she sulkily corrected herself: "I don't remember."

Around eight o'clock that evening, Christian had just turned on the television when the telephone in the entryway rang. Claire Marie froze.

"You're not going to answer it?" Christian asked.

"Yes, I am," she said without moving. "I'll get it right away." Then, in a toneless voice: "It's stopped. Surely a wrong number."

She went over to the window, raised the curtain, and stood against the glass.

"Did you see something?" Christian asked. "I've noticed that you've been standing at the window constantly of late. Are you waiting for someone?"

He stood up, raised the curtain in his turn, observed the street.

"Is it the burglary that's frightening you? It shouldn't. If we remember to lock the doors, that'll be enough. You're not running any risk."

The following day, she took Mélanie to a birth-day party. She'd had almost no sleep. The house was full of children, and she soon found the noise unendurable. She went out, heading for the Parc de Saint-Cloud, but when she saw the park gate, she turned her back on it and took some side streets, where she got lost; they had the same even slope as those in her neighborhood, the same buhrstone houses, the same well-maintained residences, all of them different, some dating from the 1930s, with their overly ornate little towers, while others were almost new and had painted doors, an English look, garden gates, large, practical garages, rain-soaked gardens. She walked on, past more and more houses. "It's all completely built up, you can't imagine the number of houses on those hills. You can't imagine," my sister said, "the number of lives. Do you ever think about that sometimes? The number of lives?"

She came to a train station on the Transilien suburban line. There were some people in the glass shelter, waiting for their train. She wanted to take it too. But finally she happened upon a telephone booth. She went in and dialed Marc Hermann's number. After the phone rang three times, the answering machine was activated: it wasn't Hermann's voice, but one of those synthetic voices that recite their lines mechanically: "You have reached an automated answering system." This discouraged her; she hesitated, decided not to leave a message (*What good would it do?*), let the tape run all the way to the end.

The trains made a lot of noise, yet she heard (or tried to hear), behind the fluctuating levels of the answering tape, the unknown life of the office where Marc Hermann currently was not, and where Marc Hermann had perhaps never been; similarly, the voice-mail recorded the vague sounds of the afternoon, the noises of the suburb, of the vehicles, of the train pulling into the station.

THE PHONE WENT DEAD. She stepped out of the booth and turned to the left.

It was cold. The farther she walked, however, the less oppressed she felt, and the better she breathed. The air was damp from the showers that were occasionally wrung out of the gray sky; there was an odor of recently soaked earth, of winter earth. The smell was so strong that my sister thought it had impregnated the silent message she'd left on the answering machine.

The streets she traversed that day reminded her of our childhood. Before, she'd never recognized the kinship between the streets of Ville-d'Avray and those of our old Brussels neighborhood, around the park in the municipality of Woluwe-Saint-Pierre. Modest beauty salons that had never been renovated, with their rows of sinks and their old-fashioned hairdressers, ladies all, reminded her of Chez Rosa, where we'd go to meet Mama. Women would be waiting in there, sitting under helmet-like hair dryers with their curlers wrapped in pink nets.

"Your mother's under the dryer," Rosa would tell us. "Come back in fifteen minutes."

"Do you recall Rosa's hair salon?" my sister asked me. "And I don't know if you remember, because you were younger, but there were Japanese cherry trees on the streets. In Ville-d'Avray, there are magnolias and

tulip trees, but never that kind of cherry tree, the ones that look like they're covered with cotton when they're in bloom; I've never seen any since. I guess it's an unusual species here. Maybe this isn't the right climate for them."

She looked at the houses with great curiosity; they seemed at once unknown and familiar; she told herself that surely, during the days when there was sunshine, it must penetrate to the centers of the various rooms and make everything more cheerful; but that day there was no sun.

She saw some shaded lamps next to certain windows, as well as the backs of some armchairs, covered with cloths, as in her own house. In some cases, decals of stars or fir trees left over from the past Christmas were still on the windowpanes, and she told herself those were kids' rooms—Mélanie too had asked permission to stick decals on her window.

Some bicycles were leaning against walls.

There must have been dishcloths hung up in the kitchens, cabinets filled with flour and sugar, machines on standby (refrigerators refrigerating, dishwashers ready for washing and drying duties).

She told herself that other women, perhaps, were moving around in the silence of those houses, behind their papered walls; she wondered if the women were bending over sideboards, putting dishes away. Or over sinks, cleaning them with a spray of some disinfecting product. Or if they were ironing and calmly placing the warm, folded articles to the right of the ironing board. Or if they were turning on televisions, just so there'd be some sound coming from somewhere. Maybe telephones were ringing, and those women were hoping that a man's voice would be on the other end of the line.

(*Where are you*, they'd say, *in a meeting? Keeping an outside appointment?*)

But often it was an advertising message. And if there was a maid working in the house, she wouldn't disturb herself; the phone wasn't for her, she knew that; it was never for her; many domestic employees were foreigners, they barely spoke French, they'd listen to the message left on the machine by a human voice, a human voice that broke and entered the silence of the empty room, leaving a message to which no other voice responded— and which was followed by the subdued, terse hum of the answering mechanism resetting itself.

———

When he came back, Hermann would surely listen to his messages; he'd hear nothing but silence, the buzz of the tape, the heavy sound of the train entering the station just at the moment when she made the call. *No message,* he'd think. He'd roll the tape again. He'd strain to hear the vague murmur of a suburban afternoon. Practically nothing. It was all that would remain to him of my sister.

The streetlamps came on all at once.

Claire Marie turned up her collar and pulled it close around her neck as she walked, and the streets succeeded one another; there were always intersections, cafés, little canteens, here and there a house higher than the others with a freshly repainted balcony, plucked, muddy gardens whose lawns were now nothing more than grass, barely finished new buildings (wet sand from the worksite and the cement mixers still remained on the lots). The building never stopped.

The streets grew darker, the lots wider and more wooded; there were more trees. Suddenly, she saw a great hole in the landscape. She said to herself, *The Ponds!*

She wasn't sure exactly how, but she'd headed toward the Fausses-Reposes Forest, and although it wasn't the best time (it's not advisable for a woman to walk alone in the vicinity of the Ponds in the evening), she kept on going.

Eventually, she found a bench and sat down facing the water; night was falling; it would probably stay cloudy, without too much wind; the thick cloud cover would stall over Paris and Ville-d'Avray. Descending airplanes were making their final approach; she could see their blinking lights. Paris's beating heart was very close, and the planes were trying to land on it.

The lights went on in the common areas of some buildings that formed an apartment complex, the last one before the forest began: a few low, numbered structures, separated by trees and streetlamps, with a letter on each entrance door and the look of public buildings.

All of a sudden, a man came out of the undergrowth opposite her; she sensed rather than saw his silhouette on the other side of the pond. He must have noticed her as well; he'd been able to "spot" her because of her light raincoat, which was brighter in the shadows, brighter than the shadows.

The man didn't move. She knew he could follow each of her movements because of the light patch she made on the dark bench. She tried to see if he had a dog;

a dog would have reassured her, would have meant that the man was simply out for a walk.

As far as she could make out, he was standing with his back to the woods, facing her. Maybe he was remaining immobile like that because he was smoking.

She shook herself, got up, and retraced her steps, heading for the lights of the apartment complex. It was inhabited, there would be people in it, around it; she walked fast, her hands in her pockets; she walked about a hundred meters, following the marked-out path, and then glanced behind her; he'd already come halfway around the pond. Maybe, when she reached the willow grove up ahead and skirted it, following its curve, she'd disappear from his view. But he was walking faster than she was.

"In the end," my sister said, "I started running; I made myself breathless. I was crying too, the way you cry only in dreams when great difficulties arise. I told myself that if I tried to call out, I wouldn't be able to make a sound. He shouted something behind me."

By *a miracle,* she found herself at the top of her street; there was light in the living-room picture window.

She'd completely forgotten Mélanie. Christian had gone to pick her up from the birthday party. And now he was giving her something to eat. He looked glum, full of reproach. The little girl was eating an egg.

"Why are you coming home so late?" Christian asked. "Where were you? Two hours I've been waiting for you!"

Mélanie thrust her spoon the wrong way into her egg and said nothing. Her face was all smeared, and the yellow egg yolk was running down onto her napkin.

My life, my sister said to herself. *Here's what I'm making of my life: this angry man, and this dirty-faced little girl.*

She stopped talking. I too remained silent. Finally, I said, "Why did you give up at the last moment? Suppose you were wrong? Maybe he was the real thing. You didn't call him again? If it had been me, I think I would have tried to find out."

"Find out what?" my sister asked.

"Who I was dealing with. If I'd been in your place, I think I would have gone up. I would have rung the doorbell of the apartment."

My sister bowed her head.

The idea that she might not have told me everything briefly crossed my mind, the idea that there was a part of the story that she was keeping to herself.

Nevertheless, I insisted: "You never saw him again?"

"No," she said with an effort. "Never. He must have telephoned several times, but I never answered. For a long time, I avoided the places where I'd met him before, I stopped going to Saint-Cloud alone. I avoided the Ponds."

"But you still think about it."

"It occurs to me sometimes, of course," said my sister.

"Who's to say that he didn't take to driving past your house? That he's not still doing that?"

With one and the same movement, the two of us looked at the black garden, the unlocked gate.

"No," said my sister. "Don't be ridiculous."

"And his import-export business?"

"I looked it up in the telephone book: there was no Hermann in Saint-Cloud; I never found even one. There was one in Versailles, but it wasn't a company, and the address didn't match the address on his card. I called the number in the telephone book once, but the woman who answered told me her husband was dead."

SEVERAL YEARS LATER, maybe five or six, Claire Marie went back to the cul-de-sac in Versailles. Nothing had changed; the same silence still pervaded the cul-de-sac.

This time she wasn't there on an early evening in winter, however, but on a day in spring, in broad daylight, and in gorgeous weather; birds were singing; the month was May; she saw that the big tree whose branches protruded over the wall was an enormous, magnificent chestnut.

The chestnut's blossoms had opened; their pale color stood out against the mass of practically black leaves. The tree seemed to be spreading, over the end of the cul-de-sac and over the garden on the neighboring property, the regal and sad splendor of time.

How many years has it been already? she mused.

She walked along to the building; the plaque was still there: DR. ZHANG—MANUAL MANIPULATION, ACUPUNCTURE.

She climbed the stairs and rang the bell on the second floor. After a few minutes, the door opened. A man who she supposed was Dr. Zhang stood before her. Behind him, the apartment was just like what she'd imagined, the kind of commonplace apartment you find in those little complexes. The office on the floor above—where she'd never been—must have been laid out according to the same plan: a rectangular vestibule with an old-style parquet floor, a hall leading to one or more rooms on the street side. The door of the examination room was half-shut. She never knew whether someone was lying on a bed in there, or whether Dr. Zhang was alone in the apartment, waiting. Maybe no one had come to consult Dr. Zhang for a long time, or maybe he'd retired and the office where he'd seen his patients was also his place of residence. Maybe the room in the back, the one that overlooked the cul-de-sac shaded by the chestnut tree, was nothing but an untidy living area where he spent most of his days.

"Do you wish to make an appointment?" he asked.

"No," she said, "I just want some information. Was there a business on the third floor, right above your office? An import-export company? It would have been five or six years ago."

To give herself a pretext, she'd taken the card with her, and now she glanced at it: "The company was called Hermann Import-Export. Did you know Monsieur Hermann?"

Dr. Zhang looked disappointed. His face hardened.

"I don't know," he said as he closed the door. "I don't see anything at all. I'm not familiar with that company. I don't spend any time with my neighbors. You must be mistaken. Good day, Madame."

The gate opened with its metallic click.

My niece flew in like a bird, graceful in her ballet flats. She sat on the grass beside us and said, "Still chatting away? You two are inexhaustible. You haven't moved? You haven't even turned on the light! All the houses around are lit up; I thought you'd gone out. You've stayed out here in the dark this whole time?"

"Yes," Claire Marie said. "Was your movie good? Where's Clément?"

"Clément left me at the end of the street—he's not coming in tonight. He's got some work to finish. The movie was very good," my niece said. "I really liked it a lot. What did you do?"

"We talked, as you see. We had a nice, peaceful visit. It was very good too. We didn't notice what time it was.

The hours went by fast. We talked about our memories of when we were young."

"About your sweethearts?" my niece asked with an indulgent little smile.

I said, "Of course. Your mother had a few, like everyone else; I particularly remember a long-haired rock'n'roller your grandfather couldn't bear to see in the house—he didn't like his hairstyle. There were some terrible scenes."

I mimicked Papa: "That boy, is he unaware that barbers exist?"

I'm very good at mimicking Papa. My niece laughed; her expression was vaguely incredulous.

"You don't know what your mother was like, you can't remember her as I do. Obviously, you didn't know her when she was young. She was a fanatical dancer." (I thought: *fanatical dreamer.*) "The kind that could dance all night long—which must seem incredible to you. That wasn't your generation. You weren't around for that era. It was before the year 2000," I said. "We didn't even have mobile phones then. Can you imagine?"

I was certain that those formulations meant nothing to Mélanie. "Before the year 2000" didn't compute; not even "Your mother was a fanatical dancer" conveyed anything; the degree of separation was too great; too much time had passed; it was only a phrase that my niece might recall later, a sequence of words that would come back to her the way some words come back when you're trying to remember, one of those phrases you hang on to when other memories fade: *Mama really liked to dance, I think. Mama just loved dancing.*

WHO REALLY KNOWS US? We say so few things, and we lie about almost everything. Who knows the truth? Had my sister really told me the truth? Who can know it? Who'll remember us? With the passage of time, our hearts will become dark and dusty, like Dr. Zhang's examination room.

A waiting room where you've been waiting your whole life. No sound from the other side. No sign.

I felt a kind of anguish. I kept asking myself, *Suppose she was wrong? Me too, who is it, what is it I'm waiting for? Who has come for me?*

The headlights of Christian's car lit up the front gate; he entered the house through the garage and came to us across the lawn.

Claire Marie now looked different, more composed— her everyday look. She seemed to remember what time it was; she stood up.

"Dinner's not ready. I should have made something. We're late. You must be starving."

She went back inside the house to turn on the lights.

"It doesn't matter," said Christian. "I'm in no hurry. Such great weather! You all were right to take advantage of it." He turned to me: "It's a surprise to see you on a Sunday."

———

He sat down; we chatted about this and that, about the summer that had gone on and on, about these transitional days, which can last until the middle of October, when the air's still muggy, when the heat can still be thick in the middle of the afternoon, about the hot winds from Spain—but the woods are full of chestnuts, and the evenings much cooler. We made banal small talk, said that the fall here in Ville-d'Avray, the early fall, had something poignant about it, something you could sense more in the suburbs than in Paris, which was cut off from the seasons. Christian said that flies were starting to get into the houses: "The garage was full of them this morning. It's because they don't have long to live."

I recited:

The dahlia puts on its cockade,
The marigold its golden toque.

Claire Marie continued:

Rain bubbles on the garden pond,
The swallows gathered on the roof
Confabulate and correspond.

Christian calmly sipped his whiskey. His day hadn't been tiring, mostly checkups for people returning from the summer break, medical certificates for the resumption of athletic activity, routine things. Patients came in to be examined for less than nothing, for *rhumatismes*, as they called them: the first *rhumes*, the first winter colds. They dawdled. They told him stories about how they'd spent their summer, about their family matters.

"You know," Christian said to me, "many of my patients have been living in this area for a long time. They're getting old; they're all too aware that nothing lasts forever; they don't expect anything, they just want things to go on as they are. They need to talk, they feel better when I give them some medicine, when they leave with their prescriptions; all they ask is to be reassured. They need me to tell them, 'Nothing serious, everything's fine.' Sometimes, that's the only point of their office visit: they want me to say, 'Nothing serious, everything's fine,' or to take their blood pressure and say, 'Your pressure's excellent'; they cheer right up—'You think so, doctor? You're sure?' I see the look on their faces when I suggest they need a little complementary examination. I'm always careful to add, 'Just to be on the safe side,' or 'A simple check.' I'm always careful to make it clear that I don't see anything worrisome."

He took Claire Marie's hand. "My dear, I still remember the look your father gave me when I told him, 'Jean-Paul, this time you really do have to see a specialist.'"

We all fell silent.

The yellow light of the streetlamp on the sidewalk shone on one side of the chestnut leaves and on my niece's blond hair as she sat there quietly on the grass, her arms crossed around her knees, and listened to us. She also appeared dreamy, she was still under the spell of the film; maybe Clément kissed her in the movie theater. She had her secrets too.

WHEN I STOOD UP, my sister protested: "You don't want to have dinner with us? Are you sure?"

"No. I have to leave now. I'll say goodbye. It's too late, Luc's going to be waiting for me. He's supposed to come home this evening. He'll ask me where I've been; he's going to think I've had some sort of dubious encounter"—I laughed—"and I'll have to tell him I went to Ville-d'Avray."

Christian and Mélanie collected the glasses and went back to the house. They entered the kitchen; we could hear them laughing; I imagined that my niece was telling her father about the rock'n'roll dancer with the long hair.

I told myself, *It wasn't anything, nobody knows about it. Nobody will ever know anything about it. Except for me. It passes, all that. It's like the wind.*

The lights and the laughter amid the dark masses of the plants in the garden demonstrated the peace of an illuminated house (*Your sister's pretty house*, as Mama used to say). A few midges were whirling in the halo around the two electric lanterns, one on either side of the door; the big lamp in the living room shed a round pool of light on the lawn. *In the end*, I told myself, *that was all the peace you can—sometimes, at certain moments—get out of life, that fragile peace, so fleeting that we're so frightened of losing it, the peace you taste on certain evenings, the feeling, so hurtful, so acute: a moment stopped, as it were, in time, a summer's end, a truce, the sounds of some voices in a garden, a lamp shining in a window.*

It was what my sister had chosen. She'd been right. I understood her. *The remnant*, I said to myself. *The dream.* I recalled the title of a novel that had dazzled me in the old days: *Les bas-fonds du rêve.*[3]

Claire Marie walked me to the gate.

Ever since the neighbor had mown his lawn, the whole street smelled of cut grass. I don't know why the smell of cut grass can give you such a feeling of sadness, and also such a violent desire to keep on living.

There wasn't the least breath of wind. The chestnut leaves that remained untouched by the light of the streetlamp were thick, damp, and unmoving, massed together in the shadows.

The gate closed behind me; my sister leaned over the top of the gate and waved to me as I drove off. That's the last image of that Sunday, my sister raising her hand above the gate, like Aunt Hélène when we were kids and Papa would come to Fromentine and pick us up at the end of summer vacation, at the end of August, and the

---

3 *Translator's Note:* Roughly, "The Lower Depths of Dream," *Les bas-fonds du rêve* is the title of a volume of fiction by the Uruguayan writer Juan Carlos Onetti (1909–1994) in French translation. The volume contains some short stories and Onetti's 1959 novel *Para una tumba sin nombre* ("A Grave with No Name").

car would pull away, always at night, and always with the trunk fully loaded, down the little street whose surface was sandy because it was very close to the dunes (in reality, it was a cul-de-sac; it ended on one of those sandy paths that cross the Pays de Monts forest).

I was sure that my sister would look in my direction until my rear lights weren't anything more than two points in the darkness, until I turned at the intersection, until all that was left to see were two lamplit sidewalks.

When I reached the Sèvres–Ville-d'Avray train station, I shot a glance at it in spite of myself; the platforms overlooking the street were deserted; no train had just arrived, no train was about to depart; the rails were visible, the coal-colored ballast, and the illuminated signboard displaying the schedules, which threw back the darkness on all sides.

That evening, the station reminded me more than it usually did of a certain movie I'd seen long before. It starts there, on the platform whose dry surface I could see above street level. Of course, the place had changed; one scene in the film shows the old metal passenger bridge with the finely worked guardrail, a span that has certainly been replaced by one of those ceramic-tile-lined corridors similar to the lanes of swimming pools;

the men are wearing hats and carrying their raincoats folded over their arms. As for Corot's Ponds in winter—which provide one of the movie's settings—you could still see them, they hadn't changed. It's there that a young man, a kind of student, takes a young girl on walks. I remembered that the actor was blond, that he had light eyes and a foreign accent (German? Russian?), and that he was a demobilized soldier back from the war—but which war? The film was a distant memory. The young man goes to the orphanage on Sundays and picks up the little girl after passing himself off as her father. Then he takes her to the Ponds. The two of them play together, and nothing more. Nobody's suspicions are aroused, nobody checks; no one besides him comes for her either, and it's normal for a father to come and pick up his little girl on Sundays and spend time with her. On Sundays, there must be great sadness in the orphanage for the children who remain shut up inside, because "anything's better than that."

Life can be a terrible orphanage, I said to myself, mentally evoking the bare trees, the muddy banks of the Ponds in Ville-d'Avray, the rare walkers, the black-and-white landscape, as if remembering the movie shed light on a great many things, as if it had a connection with my sister's story.

In the film, the little girl wears a knit cap, woolen stockings, and an overcoat with a half-belt exactly like the ones we wore, my sister and I, back in the days of Thierry la Fronde and Mr. Rochester. She's a girl of our generation.

I remembered liking that film very much; it showed Ville-d'Avray in a strange light, and it conjured up a feeling that was almost uneasy, almost fearful, because the viewer was kept wondering, *What can possibly happen? Whatever are they doing?*

The road I took ran along the wall of the Parc de Saint-Cloud. The gate was closed. Everything was dark.

I was tranquilly rolling along; the brake lights on the car in front of me kept coming on, because we were all moving in slow fits and starts. There were traffic jams on the way into Paris. I had to put my foot on the brake a lot too, and as long as I followed the wall, every time I braked, I looked at the practically impenetrable tapestry of the trees.

I thought of the little girl's secret games with the young man, and about my sister's encounters with Hermann.

When you see the film for the first time, you don't know what might be about to happen next, and then, in the end, the police kill the man!

ANOTHER THING YOU NEVER KNOW is when exactly you leave Ville-d'Avray. It's bordered by many little municipalities. Very quickly, the population density increases; the city lights replace the dark, damp expanses of the gardens; very quickly, the gaseous halo of vaguely orangish artificial light, the halo that covers peri-urban neighborhoods, begins to glow, so continuous that there are no more shadows: Suresnes, with its houses closer and closer together, its tiered buildings climbing up the hillsides, its hair salons, its mini-marts open till midnight, its pizza parlors promising quick deliveries, its driving schools displaying fees for a "point reduction course" or a "learner's permit," its cafés, closed on Sundays, their terrace chairs piled up inside.

Since I was coming down from Montretout, Paris appeared below me; it was something-o'clock sharp, I don't recall which hour, maybe ten. The Eiffel Tower was sparkling like the edges of those old Christmas cards, covered with a layer of imitation frost; the tower's beacon of blue light slowly swept the tepid sky, you could see it from everywhere, from where I was as well as from the windows of the big, silent, posh apartments on the Champ-de-Mars.

Lower down, the red rear lights of the vehicles driving out of the tunnel descended toward the Seine as if they formed a single uninterrupted stream, or flowed into a basin.

IT HAD BEEN COOL when I left my sister's. A fall chill was starting to rise out of the grass. But in Paris, on the outer boulevards, on the asphalt that the afternoon had warmed, you could find the acrid, spicy heat and the animation of summer evenings. You had the impression that you were returning to real life, swift and brutal; buses passed; people walked fast, decisively, and wore T-shirts; huge electronic movie posters shone on the boulevards. But I was coming home from another world. Before my eyes, I still had the cones of pale orange light that lit the walls of the residences on my sister's street. The silence, and all around the cool, damp blackness of the night.

I was as sad as if I'd been exiled.

Had my sister lied to me? Had she gone up to the third floor? Had she returned to the cul-de-sac, once, several times? I heard her saying to me, *Don't be ridiculous*.

WHEN LUC FOUND ME, I was sitting on the living room sofa in the dark.

"What's wrong?" Luc said. "What's the matter with you? Why haven't you turned on a light? You're making one of those faces!"

He understood right away: "You've been to Ville-d'Avray again!"

DOMINIQUE BARBÉRIS is a French novelist. Her first book, *La Ville,* was published by Arléa in 1996. Eight further books have been published by Gallimard. *Les Kangourous* was adapted for film by Anne Fontaine under the title *Entre ses mains.* *Quelque chose à cacher* won the Prix des Deux Magots and the Prix de la Ville de Nantes in 2008. In 2018 her novel *L'année de l'éducation sentimentale* was awarded the Prix Jean-Freustié / Fondation de France. Barbéris also teaches writing workshops at the Sorbonne.

JOHN CULLEN is the translator of many books from Spanish, French, German, and Italian, including Susanna Tamaro's *Follow Your Heart,* Philippe Claudel's *Brodeck,* Carla Guelfenbein's *In the Distance with You,* Juli Zeh's *Empty Hearts,* Patrick Modiano's *Villa Triste,* and Kamel Daoud's *The Meursault Investigation.* He lives on the Shoreline in southern Connecticut.